For Joan, in remembrance of stories with endings. Paul.

drogheda writes

An anthology of poems, stories and memoirs
by members of Drogheda Creative Writers and
writers from the Drogheda area

With an Introduction by Deirdre Purcell

Edited by Roger Hudson and Maggie Pinder

Drogheda Creative Writers

Published by Drogheda Creative Writers
Barlow House
Narrow West Street
Drogheda
Co. Louth
Ireland
Telephone: 041 983 0732.

© 2007 Individual Contributors

Cover Design by John Moloney
incorporating the painting *Peter Street, Drogheda 2007*
by Richard Moore

All rights reserved. No parts of this publication may be
reproduced or transmitted in any form or by any means,
including photocopying and recording, without written
permission of the publisher. Such written permission must also
be obtained before any part of this publication is stored in a
retrieval system of any nature. Requests for permission should be
directed to:
Drogheda Creative Writers, Barlow House, Narrow West Street,
Drogheda, Co. Louth, Ireland

The publishers gratefully acknowledge the assistance of
Drogheda Borough Council Arts Office,
Drogheda Concentrates Ltd., Drogheda Credit Union
and Marks & Spencer Ltd

ISBN-13: 978-0-9551556-2-8

Printed in the Republic of Ireland by ColourBooks Ltd.
105 Baldoyle Industrial Estate, Baldoyle, Dublin 13

CONTENTS

Introduction by Deirdre Purcell

It is a privilege to introduce this book dedicated to, and written by the Drogheda Creative Writers group. With 72 contributions from 38 contributors, the anthology aims to give an overview of the quality and range of poetry, short story and memoir writing going on in Drogheda and surrounding areas today, not only by members of DCW itself, but also by a selection of established writers from the town connected with the group by virtue of assisting with seminars and judging of competitions. Also included are the top four prize-winners in the most recent Amergin Creative Writing Awards who range from as far as Alaska.

And not all who write, whether poetry, drama, fiction in all its guises, or works of scholarship and research, do so to get the work into print. The authors of these pieces range from those who write for themselves, friends and family, for sheer enjoyment and self-expression, to those for whom writing is a regular occupation and part or all of their livelihood.

The ambition of many writers, however, is to be published and professional authors are frequently asked for the secret of success, for tips on how to achieve this. As the Drogheda Writers know very well, there is no secret, formulaic or otherwise, and the only tip worth hearing is to "write, write, write" – followed by "edit, edit, edit" and to keep at it, no matter what obstacles are erected or by whom.

Why do we write in the first place?

That is a true mystery, when the work can be hard and thankless and, to quote Robert Louis Stevenson: "How little does [a reader] consider the hours of toil, consultation of authorities, researches in the Bodleian, correspondence with learned and illegible Germans – in a word, the vast scaffolding that was first built up and then knocked down, to while away an hour for him in a railway train."

There are joys, undoubtedly, when the work sings, when, having settled in to write for an hour or so, you find on consulting your watch

1

some time later that six hours have passed. And, for writers of fiction such as myself, the ultimate reward in creating a fictional world lies in the anticipation that others may choose (or not!) to enter it for enjoyment, and perhaps illumination.

The majority of a writer's time, however, involves wrestling with our individual sentences and paragraphs. We torture ourselves to ascertain if this thought we have sought to convey is not only apt but clear – or if we have obscured it with too many writerly flourishes. We work and re-work that lyrical passage for fear we might be showing off – or, worse, might irritate the reader who wants to get on with the story. We finish today's work and, on viewing it tomorrow, are impelled to throw it away in disgust and start all over again. But we continue to write for the same reason that all artists attend to their art: because they are responding to a deep urge to create.

When work is especially tough for me, I re-read a quote I have on my desk from a Native American author, Darcy McNickle, in his book, *Wind from An Enemy Sky*: Here is part of it:

"To be born was not enough. To live in the world was not enough. One had to reach . . . to reach with his mind into all things, the things that grew from small beginnings and the things that stayed firmly placed and enduring. . . "

That is what we writers do. We reach.

Congratulations to the DCW.

Deirdre Purcell.
Mornington, February 2007.

A Note from the Editors

Drogheda Creative Writers has published anthologies of its members' work before, usually photocopied and stapled painstakingly by hand – an achievement to produce at the time and successful in reaching fellow Droghedians. Now, with nineteen years of survival and mutual support as a group behind it and with the backing of the Drogheda Borough Council Arts Office (which didn't exist then) and local concerns, we are launching a more ambitious enterprise with this volume *Drogheda Writes*, one we hope may be repeated in the future.

We would like to congratulate all our contributors on the high standard of their writings and having the courage to submit. To any local writers who did not hear about the venture in time, our regrets and hopes that they will have another opportunity in the future.

We hope you all gain as much enjoyment from reading this amazing variety of talent as we have from editing it.

Roger Hudson and Maggie Pinder

About Drogheda Creative Writers

The Drogheda Creative Writers group is a mutual support group of writers and would-be writers, which meets on the first and third Tuesday of each month (with a break midsummer and at Christmas) at Barlow House, Narrow West Street, Drogheda. New members are always welcome.

Some meetings feature a specific talk or topic of discussion, others are more informal but all include ample time for the lifeblood of the group: members reading their work, sharing it for praise and helpful comment under the supportive umbrella of fellow writers who rapidly become friends – the craic is good too.

We find we learn a lot from one another and our own work develops positively, with helpful tips on different aspects of the writing art and business from more experienced members. Occasional open sessions provide a chance to read work in front of an audience and special seminars an opportunity for learning more formally. DCW members also played a leading role in last September's Amergin Literary Festival.

Amergin Creative Writing Awards

2007 sees the revival of the Amergin Creative Writing Awards now in their 15th year, after skipping last year. Having built it up from a small local affair to one of the most successful Irish literary competitions, attracting entries from all round the globe, the DCW is pleased to welcome the involvement of Drogheda Borough Council Arts Office and Droichead Arts Centre in ensuring the future of the Awards. The prizewinning entries featured on pages 55 to 63 demonstrate the high standard the competition achieves.

Bernadette Smyth

KISSING

She prided herself on her kissing. Long before she knew what sex was, she'd kissed. Long rain-drenched ones with friends, copying the movie kisses they saw on television, suction-filled ones like the smack of a wrist. That's how she learned. Learned to give good kisses. The kind she gave to people who deserved them. The kind she hoped they talked about afterwards. The kind that made their lust reach all the way down to their toes and left them hopeful, expectant. The long, slow, luscious kind.

She loved the wonder of each kiss; loved how sometimes it was the flirtatious velocity of a fan opening with the tiniest movement, sometimes the thick flap of an eagle jumping off the highest branch of a tree, sometimes the delicate humming of a lullaby fading out.

She kissed in the alleyway behind her house, with the girl next door who now avoided her. Marion. With an O. And what an O she pouted when she wanted those lip caresses, what a charm GiGi found in withholding, or with teasing, or with making rules around the kisses. You must keep your hands by your side. If you move them, I'll stop. The girl, Marion-with-an-O, standing there with her eyes closed in the alleyway behind their houses, her arms by her side, her lips pointing out as far as possible. Open your eyes. Nothing. Open your eyes. Nothing. She leaned in and kissed, soft, gently. Open your eyes. If you don't, I'll stop. Marion-with-an-O's eyes opening, blinking, as if wishing it could be anyone but GiGi in front of her, yet unable to walk away. Yet. Look at me. *Marion with the O lips, the O eyes now open, staring hard at the distance past GiGi.* Look at me. Into my eyes.

Nothing.

Or I'll stop. Hazel eyes, furtively catching brown ones. GiGi leaning in again, placing her face up close, touching her lips against the O of Marion's, biting the edges. Marion's O eyes closed, arms still by her side.

You closed your eyes. That's it. No more.

Ah, the power of a kiss.

It never changed. Long after the afternoon at the mall, after GiGi went up to Marion-with-an-O, touched her on the shoulder, saw the panic in her eyes as she glanced around; long after she heard the Oh! of dismissal, saw the shrug of her shoulder, felt the push of her arm. Oh, it's you. Long after she heard the others' laughter, the whispered name. Generous GiGi. Not because she gave gifts, but because she had a Name. A Name. An embarrassment for Marion.

Long after all that, she still loved to kiss.

The kisses she gave to get gifts were different than the ones she gave as gifts. Marion-with-an-O had been given a gift, a kiss full of softness and tenderness and desire. A fully wrapped piece in itself, with no need for further gifts to make it complete. Enough for even the most deserving O.

The kisses she gave to get gifts were calculated, coming out of a place of need. They worked best on men, which was why she kept the selfless gift kisses for women. Men's lips were different. They were sure of themselves, pushing rather than pouting, demanding rather than requesting. When women's lips demanded, they did so like spoilt children, trying to get what they want in the only way they knew how, but not really sure they will – or even if they deserve it. Men's lips demanded in a way that expected results, that never contemplated the possibility of real failure. Not many women kissed like that.

The men loved innocence. She played the game, flirting first with her eyes, catching them in bars or on trains or buses, looking as innocent as possible. That was the trick, really. It had worked for her for so long. Innocence. She sometimes wore a red hat, a beret two sizes too large and with the elastic stretched at the edges. It sat on her long chestnut hair loosely, sometimes sitting this way, sometimes that. A little too big, but it never failed. It made her look vulnerable, having a hat that misfitting, and they loved it. It pulled the strongest feelings from them, so that kissing was really only a confirmation.

She was good at creating desire, weaving illusions around their lips like tiny spider webs of yearning, until she reached the edges of their passion, and then stepped back, adjusting her red hat.

She kissed differently in the red hat.

Sometimes, when she kissed, she wanted to bite. Not those soft nibbling bites she loved to give as gifts, the ones in which she followed the indented trail with the tip of her tongue, letting it lick the inside soft edges between lips and teeth. Sometimes she wanted to bite chunks off, a hard snapping of her teeth on the softness between them.

In the alleyway behind their houses, Marion-with-an-O would pick up a piece of broken glass, lean against the high wall and trace her wrist with the sharp point, her eyes all the time on GiGi. Each day, a different colour glass. Often, she'd drag the jagged edge alongside the uplifted blue vein in her wrist, rub across the top, down the other side, the vein like the indented trail GiGi sometimes left on Marion-with-an-O's bottom lip. Once, Marion-with-an-O pressed down slightly, the sharp edge of the glass pushing against the blue of the vein. GiGi watched the vein move out of the shard's way, an unexpected avoidance. Enchanted, she reached forward to touch it, her fingernail brushing along the side of the glass. She looked for a moment at Marion. Marion with the O lips, the protruding veins. She pushed the glass aside, touched the veins, leaned her face in close to run her tongue over the indentation, loving the feel of it, sensing the pulse beneath, feeling the life of Marion in her tongue.

The slither down to wanton is soft, scarlet, soundless.

She used to kiss her stepfather, a long time ago. Quick, hard kisses, the sound of a dictionary slamming shut. Whisssshhh. Twang. The loud rush of it close to her face, drying her eyes. Lips on parchment, sticking there momentarily, leaving tiny scars on the edges of her lips that blossomed into weeping sores before they disappeared. Give your father a goodnight kiss. He, waiting expectantly, so willing to kiss her. *He's not my father.* Her mother's defence, her usual defence: Don't be cheeky and do as you are told. A child's duty to kiss strangers.

The kisses she gives the probing priest are not kisses, per se, but kisses nevertheless. Imprints of kisses, touches of them in the air above his head, his face. *Bless me, father, for I have sinned. I have kissed.* Polished oak walls surround her, caressing her arms, her shoulders, her lower back. You must confess, he says. Tell me what you do. His questions are clear, pointed, explicit. She closes her eyes and says, *I wet my lips. That's the first thing I do. I let my tongue run over my lips, paying attention to the dry spots.* Then . . .? he asks. *I kiss,* she says. She can feel his discomfort, his yearning, almost as if his lips were with her. She can feel his reluctant disapproval. She says, *I lean in and let my lips touch theirs.*

7

She kissed her stepfather until she was thirteen; planted them like weeds on his cheek until one drizzly night, on a long cold black road, the darkness lit only by the weak lights of his old car, Brose Woods on either side – haunted, scary Brose Woods – the only sound, the engine, whirring noisily, a kind of lulling sound. Then, then, the car jerking, in synch with his foot on the accelerator. Then he, proclaiming the car faulty. She, feeling something – fear? – saying, *Try to keep it going.* He, pulling onto the side of the road, saying, No point. No point. Let it rest awhile.

In the silence of the cubicle, she can hear a soft rustle, a minute movement which echoes off the low roof and softly ricochets into her lap. She remains quiet, forces the probing priest to ask, Then what? She waits again. Is that it? he asks, a note of disappointment and dismissal in his voice. He has no absolution to give her; she has not warranted any. *No*, she says. Go on, he says, his face leaning into the wire mesh, his ear whispering against it, to hear the kisses she gives him. *Then I lick, she says. With my tongue. I push it inside their mouth, touching all the soft spots, the wet spots, my lips on theirs. . .* What she describes is the kiss she gives to get gifts, for the selfless gift kiss is too precious to be given to the probing priest. A Novena, he declares, triumphant. A full Novena. She sits with her hands in her lap, smiles. It is too delicious, more than she could have anticipated. A kiss of absolution.

They waited in the car.
    And then he was leaning over her, grabbing her, and she tried to push him away, but he had a strong grip on her wrist, and she said, *Please, please, start the car,* and he said, There's something wrong with it, and she was crying as she tried to push herself against the passenger door, but by now he had undone his pants, and had pulled her to him and asked, Do you know what this is for? and she shouted, *No!* and tried to pull away, and he grabbed her shoulders and was pulling her towards him, trying to kiss her, and she could smell the whiskey and the beer and his bad breath and she said, *Please?* but he just ignored her and began pulling at her dress; and he pulled her body towards him now with his one dirty fist, the other fumbling with her underwear, and she screamed, *No!* and managed to pull away from him and it so surprised him that he lost his grip on her for a moment. A moment!

She tore her fingers scratching for the door handle, threw herself out the opening door, landing on the road, and scrambled to her feet, running all the while, tripping, tears flying past her ears, not looking behind for a long time, a minute, until she realised he wasn't following her. She slowed a little and breathed.

And then the sounds of the woods crept in, slinking through her pores with the rain. She could hear, she swore she could hear, soft screechy voices; she could smell the pine, the swamp; she could taste the darkness, the fear, the thick air; a mist like a banshee ahead of her, around her; below, a breeze, like fingers, on her ankles, tugging at her socks, her shoes, tripping her up, making her stumble, fall.

A rumble, a roar, the car starting up, the lights approaching faster than she could run, pulling up beside her, driving slowly to keep up. Get in! Nothing will happen. She ran alongside, being so scared that he would drive off and leave her there alone on the haunted road that she didn't shout No! immediately, and he said, again, Nothing will happen. She stopped and stared at him, but he looked away, said, Get in. And suddenly she understood what people meant when they talked about choosing the devil you know over the devil you don't, and hoped she made the right choice.

And by the time they got home, a silent cold drive, she began to understand something about him. By the time he said, No need to tell anyone about this? she knew that she held a kind of power over him, that his almost-realisation of his desire for her had shaken him, that she would never promise not to tell. That now he feared her. That now she was safe.

Some kisses, she knows, are the soft loss of vacuum in a leaky pipe, long and slow at the end, with a hint of noise. Many are like losing faith, slow and gradual and revealing. Some are even like rocking back and forth on her bed, feeling life lifting up inside and choking her. Others, she thinks, are like days that are night all day, all day.

Susan Connolly

PIANO LESSONS

1. Mrs MacAllister

Early September, first lesson
with Mrs MacAllister.
"Let me hear you play.
Play your favourite piece for me."
Shy, shaky, in slow motion
I try *The Sunbeam Polka*.
She nods and smiles.
I notice her man-size hands,
the kindness in her voice.

Tuesday lunchtime, Mrs MacAllister;
my name on a brand new
Grade III book.
She plays six pieces.
"Choose three you like."
We begin: right hand, left hand,
hands together, fingering.
"Though the notes are important,
feeling is everything."

2. Piano Lessons

Notes fall beneath my hands
like flame-coloured leaves.
I want to play with them,
to catch, kick, scatter
and gather them.
Eleven years old, homesick,
I crave the familiar.

Christmas over, hands
and heart numb,

10

one Tuesday lunchtime
I begin Bartok's
Slovakian Folk Tune.
The first chord sends
a shiver up my spine.

I glance sideways
at Mrs MacAllister.
"Did I play the right notes?"
"That's a minor seventh
chord," she says.
"I'll change
the fingering for you."

What a strange sound
I hold captive in my hands.
What luck to reach out
and find exactly
what I need!
At home at last in the new
and unfamiliar.

My life a piece of music
I have barely begun
to play, week by week
Mrs MacAllister draws out
the silence at my core.
Teacher and child
each Tuesday lunchtime

side by side,
with a sudden pang I know
that's my favourite piece of all.
Memory which lightens
and brightens everything.
Heartwarming, comforting
music at my core.

RAISING RUCTIONS |

We didn't know it then,
but the moment we set off
on our separate paths
away from each other,
the great search began,
like roots reaching down
into dark, damp earth,
roots no one could see,
least of all, ourselves.

One night someone
spoke your name,
asked if I knew you.
In silence
I looked at a full moon.
Then something missing
for many years
clicked back into place,
and I felt at peace.

Remembering two girls
who set up obstacles
on the school stage
and spent hours
jumping over them,
I saw how well
we took care of each other,
making the most
of a bad thing.

Running riot,
raising ructions, barred
from speaking
we sent notes.
We sought each other out,
put down roots

to steady our spirits
wherever
we might roam.

Back then
we felt that we were
playthings of the gods,
at their mercy,
prey to every little whim.
We learned from them
a simple lesson:
how to wrest fun
out of our lives.

I see us still —
two girls on a stage,
and remember the night
two paths converged
under moonlight
at the mention of your name,
I silently thinking:
How high the moon,
how very high the moon!

MORNINGTON |

Past all the bright
new houses,
down the last
wild road,
we stand on
mussel shells,
watch beacon
lights flash
green, red.

High tide,
the pilot boat,
ships crossing
the sand-bar;
stars shine
their promise
on our lives.

Nuala Early

SEÁN

A frightened little boy buried his face in the blankets, trying to muffle the sobs that shook his body. His tears forced their way through his tightly shut eyes and formed a wet patch on his pillow. Lost and frightened, everything was strange in this alien place. He had nothing to hold onto. All that was familiar, even "Teddy Padge", was no more.

He wanted Teddy Padge, and he wanted him now. Mammy always gave him Teddy Padge to help him sleep. Keep the bogies away, she always said, as she kissed him goodnight. But now, he did not know how to cry out for him in this cold place.

He peeped out of the blankets. Maybe it was all a dream. Yes, that was it. He was dreaming. Mammy was in the kitchen. He cried out in his native tongue but the silence mocked him. No Mammy, no Teddy Padge.

The hundred beds formed long, neat rows on the naked floorboards, each containing a small body. The tall, grey walls were covered in strange shadows. The Georgian windows hung like huge paintings, each square framing its own portrait of the night. Moonlight streamed through the curtainless windows, casting confusing patterns across the great room.

The silence was broken only by the sound of fretful sleep from the other children trapped in their own isolation. Seán could give neither voice nor understanding to the loneliness that consumed him as he closed his eyes, squeezing them tightly, demanding his dreams to come.

Slowly, out of the darkness, the pictures came. He could see and feel Donegal's Golden Shores. The cool, clear waters caressed his little body, and the warm sun shone brightly in the blue sky. His Mammy close by. The twinkling sound of her laugher filled the bright summer's day, as she paddled in the blue sea. He held the pictures, feeling a love and warmth enveloping his being. Slowly, slowly, he drifted into the picture and accepted the compassion of sleep's oblivion.

"Up, you lazy little pig!"

Seán started at the voice of the matron. He opened his eyes and stared up at her. To him, it seemed her face was carved in stone.

Her cold eyes pierced through him without the slightest hint of compassion. "Get up, do you hear, or are you deaf as well as dumb?"

Seán did not answer as his Gaelic tongue locked him in a silence that copper-fastened his isolation. No one understood him in this English-speaking world into which he had been so cruelly thrust.

Moving slowly, he felt the warm, wet bed beneath him. Oh, please, God, don't let her find out. Please, please.

Coming back, she poked him sharply with her short, fat fingers. "Do you hear me, you lazy article?" she shouted, as she moved to her next victim.

Slipping out of bed and turning the covers, Seán saw the now familiar yellow stain, and the helplessness of his body filled his nostrils with disgust.

Regimental lines of boys slowly made their way to the dining room. Sitting at the great wooden table, he stared at the unappetising meal of grey porridge, watery cocoa, and black bread scraped with margarine. His Mammy always cooled and sugared his porridge, and spread his bread with lovely country butter. Oh, how he missed his Mammy; why did she have to go to Heaven?

I love you, Mammy. God has plenty of Mammies, why take mine? Please, God, let me be with my Mammy. I promise I will be a good boy, I won't wet your bed and Mammy will look after me.

"Seán O'Brien!" The large figure of the matron loomed over him, causing him to shake. "Well, Seán O'Brien, is our food not good enough for you? There is a war on, you know, or is Donegal too thick to know about it? What about the poor black babies in Africa? Live with them and you will go hungry. Come up here, where we can all see you."

Grabbing him by the ear, she marched him up the room, where he saw the now familiar chair waiting. He knew what was coming. *Mammy, don't let her do it. Please, please.*

Standing him up on the chair, the matron barked at the other children to be quiet. She disappeared, only to reappear with a white bundle held at arm's length. The children fell silent, thankful that today it was some other poor unfortunate that was at her mercy.

As she draped the wet sheets around the little boy, a hundred childish voices chanted, "Seán O'Brien, piss the bed! Seán O'Brien, piss the bed!"

Staring at the floor, he let the warm tears run. He remembered his home in Donegal. But most of all, he remembered the voice telling him his Mammy was dead. Only now did he understand what dead meant.

Alone, that's what dead meant.

Alone on a chair.

Alone in this terrible place.

Alone with his sadness and shame.

Dead meant that he would never know the comfort of love's sweet harbour again.

John "Dixie" Nugent

DISCO FLU

You have got Disco Flu
Strange as it seems,
Flares and hairs on your chest
Medallions with whacking hips

To a beat they are playing your song
Flying in your face with
Flashing lights colourful thighs

This is what makes you tick
Like a clock you ring your chimes

Never look back 'til age grinds
You to a halt
Just whack those hips
Let everyone take the piss

Strange as it seems in a surreal sense
No jab is going to cure this sickness

Just more dancing.

| THE BALKANS

There is a war
And Milosevic is evil,

There is a war
And NATO is an accomplice,

There was a limb
Joined to a torso,

There was a family
But father was slaughtered,

There were tears but shouts of downed
Planes make newspapers headlines,

There is a war
May God forgive us.

There is nothing except intransience
Only the smell of death,

There is nothing to gain
From owning clay and flag.

THE TIGER |

The Tiger Economy is still tearing
At my throat,
Teasing me with designer dinners,
As my belly rumbles hunger,
On the road to homelessness the
Tiger is munching my entrails,
In its greedy lust for satisfaction
We are left wanting.
This world, and now our country
Stinks of capitalist doctrines.
The river beckons
But I will change your selfish ways
And shoot you down
Celtic Tiger.

SADIE |

Scintillating Sadie is so salacious
With a chakra to match
Her celestial welcomes are legendary
But lo and behold those who fall foul, carrying the book of life
She fashions herself on the two Marys,
One a virgin, the other a high-class hooker
Who redeems herself called Magdalene,
Scintillating Sadie, I love her to bits,
But not in a hanky-panky sort of way,
You see, I have been chastised by this pure Christian
For lewd looking at her voluptuous
Curves.

Teddy Doyle

VERA'S KITCHENS

My friend Vera had two kitchens. One was down two steps at the back of the house, the other was directly above, off the first floor landing. When things got out of hand in one, Vera simply moved to the other, where the chaos of her previous occupancy had dissipated. All it needed was a quick spring clean, light the fire, and the kitchen lived. Until that, in its turn, became totally cluttered and she moved back to the other.

I used to flit between Dublin and London in the same way. Whenever life got too much in one capital, I moved to the other. "Going to find myself" I used to call it, but the thing about finding yourself is that you are there all the time. When you realise this, the real problem is accepting yourself, warts and all.

There always seemed to be people in Vera's kitchen, and, as she was a theatrical wardrobe mistress, most were of that profession. It was a place to bring your troubles and your joys. Around the big kitchen table, we raised many a glass to toast success, or to ease the pain of failure.

Vera's kitchen was also her workroom. You found a seat by moving bundles of scrap material used to patch, enhance or create many of the costumes that came from Vera's sewing machine, or you found a perch among the festoons of damp costumes when every electric fire, Super Ser and blow-heater in the house was brought in, in a desperate attempt to dry them in time for the Monday night's performance.

When times were hard there was always something to eat at Vera's table. She was an excellent cook and could not be put off, even by a lack of ingredients. I have hilarious memories of an impromptu and mysterious curry created from whatever could be found in the cupboards. I don't remember how it tasted but I know we ate it, washed down by the wine of laughter.

And there was always laughter in Vera's kitchen, like when she told us about the Saturday morning she got up late. As usual she lit a cigarette, and made herself a mug of tea, which she placed on the mantelpiece among her teen-age daughter's make-up which was spread out in front of a large, framed mirror.

Absent-mindedly she began to apply makeup to her left eye, selecting colours at random and as she warmed to her task, the design, based roughly on a peacock's feather, became more exaggerated. Adding curlicues and arabesques, fantasy was rampant. Her imagination soared like the smoke from her cigarette. She had done all she could to the left eye and was about to start work on the right, when suddenly she remembered the sandals – she had been asked to exchange them for a larger pair in time for that afternoon's matinee.

In a flurry of panic she tried to remember what she had done with them the night before. After a hectic search, which only added to the chaos of the kitchen, they were located. Kicking off her slippers, she found a pair of street shoes and grabbed a coat, which she threw on as she ran to catch a bus into town. In her anxiety, she did not notice the amused stares from her fellow passengers, or the puzzled look on the conductor's face.

When she got to the shop, she was so relieved that she prattled away to the young man who was serving her, not noticing his lack of response. Poor chap – he has probably had a jaundiced view of theatrical types ever since.

Having finished her business, Vera returned home. When she caught sight of herself in the mirror, she was hit with the full horror of what had happened. She relived the entire journey in a flash. The odd looks from her fellow passengers, the nudges, and winks, the reserved manner of the bus conductor. And she cringed as she remembered how she had chattered away to the shop assistant. She would never be able to face him again.

Dear, beloved, warm-hearted, witty, chaotic Vera, who, as she reduced her current kitchen to total disarray, also turned it into the centre of the universe, where she displayed her very special talent, the ability to accept other people as she accepted herself, warts and all.

Paul Murray

THE OPEN SECRET GARDEN

I shall not sway or surrender easily to parting from this place, for it is here that my heart knows the hope others refer to as heaven. This tiny patch of earth, known as Listoke, during the change of seasons throughout the year mirrors life within me and without me.

Sharing this space and hallowed ground with fellow creatures, I sometimes sit and listen for the choir of song carried along on gentle evening breezes. Then during intimate moments that are compounded by peace and calm, the garden speaks softly as if in whispered tones at half light, and ultimately assures me that Mother Nature herself is pleased that I retire within these walls; but then where else would I be found but here?

Lost in time amid the company of perfectly structured natural selections, the light not yet diminished heightens the full bloom of white cherry tree blossoms against the darkening greens and rough-skinned layers of tree trunks. Then quietly passing by, almost unobserved, the ghosts with whom I will one day stroll these gardens are those who have loved this place before me, and now return to walk again in the light and shade of late evening sunlight.

So before day surrenders to night, in my heart I will silently plead to the lender of this life not to recall it from me too soon, for love is a notion propagated during dreaming and I have no desire to be awakened.

For Patricia.

KILMAINHAM 1916 |

I will remain here for the present
and perhaps for a short time to come.
Then I will leave this place and go to a
designated area not of my own choosing.
With both my hands bound at the wrists,
I will walk restricted within the parade
of uniforms that identify my captors as
strangers in my own homeland.

I know that I shall be led from a room
along a corridor with stone floors where
the air is always foul and damp and
lingers heavily in the sparse light of early morning.
It is this light that takes from the dark
empty spaces the last glimmer of hope
and redemption in a place where men
and women await their fate in the certain
knowledge that a life once fuelled by
brotherhood will soon end beneath the
flag of oppression and cruel adversity.

The feeling taught en-route to the barred
window of a door leading out onto an
execution yard is one of misapprehension.
For out there, I shall stand without identity,
alone, proud and free.
A witness to the changes in my own
land in my own time and of my own doing.

In final moments, I shall not waver from
loyalty to my comrades and my cause.
And before the force of bullets from
rifles aimed toward me discharge, I will
wait in the dark silence at this early
morning hour behind a blindfold and
fail to read the eyes of the men who are

about to execute me. But in that time I
shall think of those I leave behind.

Praying to my god and drowning in
feelings of helplessness, I shall offer my
soul for redemption. I will then await the
moment that I depart this earthly place
and enter into another world that I feel
sure is promised and where the tender
loving presence of my god will embrace me.

| BLUE ROOM

Morning breaks and once again sunlight
enters through the lace-curtained
window of my room.
Locked within a tormented state of mind
remain hidden and regressed
the secrets of my womb.
Blue Room.

I lie on my bed, senses tightened.
Night hours again arrive too soon.
He comes
creeping like a serpent of inevitable doom.
Deep Blue Room.

Feel the crawling of his hands,
my mind quirks and twists.
I am helpless.
Unable to dissuade the act he is about to perform.
I go to a place at the top of my mind.
And there I wait and hide.
He stays too long.
And I, a child helpless.
Dark Deep Blue Room.

Helen Cooney

POEM (NOT PROSE)

"The McGuffin," he called it.
And they all want it.
Prose. All forms. Novel, greatest and least.
But plot won't thicken into something at all.
No McGuffin, nothin'.
Not for me. Not from me.
(Like Didi and Gogo) Not I.
And then:
The "auteur" of autism
Reading the *Arcadia* (annotated version, mark you).
Absurd! That copia of words. How could he?
That's the question. We shall see.
One of the best said the rest was silence –
When it wasn't.
Later he said: "Patience smil'd extremity out of joint."
All from a word: *patior* – two kinds now, he saw. Gloria.
So then:
He had the real McGuffin; couldn't be better; lacked for nothing there.
But then saw it lacked . . . nothing; doing nothing.
Hope then. For me. No plot necessary to apply.

VERSE

I say: clothe the naked text.
But covert or overt (poetry)? As you will.
Dress the tree; or let armed branches stand free, against the sky.
As you like it.
Thesaurus or anxiety-house? You choose.
But the word-hoard is mine. All of it. And I shall use it
As I will.
(Annaliviaplurabelle.)

Tom Winters

SCENES FROM CAFÉ LIFE
I – BATTLE
OF THE GLUTTONS

During the forties and into the fifties, a lot of Killgriffin's social life revolved around Luigi Faloona's café. Restaurants and cafés were few and Faloona's was the only one that opened late of an evening, so it became a Mecca for the younger folk of the town. A man of immaculate manners, Luigi was never known to lose his temper, even with the inevitable drunks. Customers were invariably welcomed with a delightful smile and the words, "Good evening, Sir" or "Good evening, Madam".

In those hard times, the menu was restricted. Italian ice cream, Bovril and cream crackers and, the speciality of the house, egg and chips, popularly known as "egg suppers". Friday and Saturday nights were the busiest times, after the cinema and pubs closed, when the café was packed with customers buying a takeaway or having a sit-down supper. The cubicles were generally full, each seating up to six, with all the condiments laid out on the marble-topped tables; a haven of delight and warmth in those years.

Sometimes great feats of gluttony occurred, and it was not uncommon for young men to eat five or six egg suppers. One particular Saturday night, Mick Connor, a tough building worker in his twenties with a gargantuan appetite, challenged George Fulham, a permanently hungry railway worker, as to who could eat the most, the loser to pay for the lot.

The first four or five were easy going, gobbled up with relish, and then there were two more. Luigi would shout over the counter to his brother Alfredo and sister Maria, who did the cooking, "Two mora supper please", in his beautiful Italian accent.

As the pace became slower after seven each, a new bottle of vinegar was called for. George liked his chips well soaked whereas Mick was more of a salt man. By the time they had finished their ninth, a large crowd had gathered around their table and bets were laid on the outcome. Mick was lagging behind; it was now George: ten suppers;

27

Mick: nine. Lar Flynn, a well-known punter who would bet on the proverbial two flies climbing up a wall, offered even money on George. He had plenty of takers.

It was now George's turn to slow up; he was struggling with his yolk, feeding his mouth like a baby, slowly chewing every chip. On his twelfth plateful, the sweat was dripping off him as he began to choke. Luigi, keeping an eye on things, shook his head muttering, "Craza, craza, Irish."

George called for water but it didn't help. George had had enough. He slumped back in his seat like a bloated pig. Lar was mad as he grabbed a hold of him and shook him violently, shouting, "Come on you useless bollocks, get another few down you." But it was no good, George had had enough.

The flash of victory written on his pudgy cheeks, Mick did a gluttonous lap of honour, fourteen, fifteen, sixteen, laid down his knife and fork, wiped a large hand over his greasy lips and triumphantly announced, "Give my compliments to the cook, Luigi."

When George came round, he asked Luigi for the bill.

"Twenty eight suppers at one shilling and sixpence each, that will be four pounds twenty pence, please, sir."

George handed him a five-pound note.

"You craza Irish," said Luigi.

And he handed him two pound back, and a couple of Bovrils on the house. A real gentleman with an ever-ready smile.

Those years were the golden years of Faloona's café. Many of the couples that went there for Bovril and cream crackers shared meals for the rest of their lives. It was a great meeting place for boy and girl; in those straitened times, sitting on the shining wooden seats, admiring the colourful ceramic walls, with their large mirrors was, for us, like sitting in the Ritz. Luigi, with his pearly teeth and dark Italian hair, standing there immaculate in his short white jacket, made you feel like a millionaire when he asked "What'a you like, Sir? What'a you like, Madam?"

| II – PARENT POWER

Later in the fifties, another Italian café opened called the Modena. A leading interior designer was responsible for its stylish murals depicting scenes from the Roman Empire, its art nouveau chairs and tables covered with tastefully patterned table cloths; it all seemed the height of elegance and sophistication. Patronised by the offspring of Killgriffin's wealthier families, the rowing club crowd and tennis set, it was the meeting place of smartly dressed young men and most of the glamorous young women of the town.

Eating habits were changing: it was now steak and chips, mixed grills, Fruit Melba and Knickerbocker Glory ice creams and mouth-watering homemade pastries all served by neatly dressed waitresses.

The Modena was run by the suave Giovanni Maglioggi, whose charm was palpable, and his rather distant wife Eva. The local girls adored Giovanni, who was constantly compared with Cesar Romero and Don Ameche – popular Latin American film stars of the period.

The prettiest girl ever to grace the Modena was Claire Scott the seventeen-year-old daughter of William Scott, verger of St Mark's church. A girl of rare beauty with a statuesque body, every young man in Killgriffin dreamed of dating her but her strict father kept a close watch on her, making sure she was home early at night.

Every Saturday night after the early picture show in the local cinema, Claire and her friend, Susan Wilson, would go to the Modena, where they would generally have an assortment of pastries and coffee. Giovanni would fuss over her, asking about her mama and papa and, out of politeness, those of Susan as well.

William Scott was always worried Claire would meet bad company and become like his estranged wife Rosa, who frequented the town's bars, disgracing him by mixing with low company and having a succession of lovers. He was determined that Claire, his only child, who was attending the local grammar school, would go on to Trinity College and have a good career.

Larry Bradley and his pals, Ray Farrell and Chump Smith, were regular patrons of the Modena. Larry was a good-looking fellow, about nineteen years of age with thick black hair and an engaging smile. He fancied Claire, though, as an apprentice mechanic in the local bus garage, Larry was hardly what Claire's father would consider a suitable suitor. Nevertheless he wrote romantic notes to her, and got Chump to deliver them.

Neatly written, the notes would vary depending on the latest film Larry had seen. After viewing Gary Cooper in *Beau Geste,* a story about the foreign legion, he wrote: "Dear divine angel, With a broken heart, I depart to join the Foreign Legion next week and a life of hardship and danger. Now is your last chance to go out with me and save your admirer from this fate. If you care, please meet me outside the Post Office at eight o'clock Monday night." When he saw *Blood and Sand,* he wrote, "I go to Spain, dear one, to train as a matador, drawn by the call of danger and death. Please meet me before your brave admirer meets his end in some faraway Spanish bullring." Claire and Susan would giggle when Chump delivered the little notes. Claire was pleased to have an admirer, although she never did meet him.

One Saturday night, Claire caused a sensation when she walked into the Modena escorted by Brian O'Meara, a flamboyant married man, who owned a garage in Benburb Street. No film star could have made a more glamorous entrance. With her long blonde hair and her beautifully shaped lips covered in dark vermillion lipstick, she made Lana Turner look jaded. Suddenly, the unspoiled young girl was a sophisticated woman whose every movement spelt class.

Larry Bradley and his pals were dumbfounded. The sight of their dream girl with O'Meara, the town's Casanova, left them shell-shocked.

"Just like her old one," said Chump. "She must be laughing at your silly notes. That O'Meara will give her a good time; he's loaded. Your wages wouldn't keep her in ice cream."

"Shut your mouth," said Larry, realising that his slim chance of a date with Claire was now non-existent.

When Giovanni approached Claire's table, he greeted her warmly, but, never having liked O'Meara, completely ignored him. To impress Claire, O'Meara ordered duck with orange sauce, a new addition to the menu, and also the most expensive.

As she sat there enjoying the meal and O'Meara's adoration, Ray turned to Larry and challenged him to send her a note. "Why don't you tell her about *Flying down to Rio*, that film we saw last night? You can ask her to fly away with you on your flying machine," he sniggered.

"The only notes that one is interested in is pound notes," said Chump. "She'll be up to her knees in them with O'Meara. You haven't a chance."

The following Saturday night Claire made another regal entrance to the Modena. She looked even more glamorous dressed in an expensive polka dot black dress, dangling gold earrings and high-heeled shoes. As Larry watched her, she personified all the dream girls he had ever seen, a mixture in his imagination of Ingrid Bergman in *For Whom the Bells Toll*, Jane Russell in *The Outlaw* and Hedy Lamarr in *Tantalaya*.

O'Meara ordered fillet steak "rare" for both of them. Then, just as they were starting their dessert of ice-cream and fruit, Claire's father burst into the café, his face livid with rage and his eyes smouldering with contempt as he gazed at his beloved daughter making a fool of herself with a married man.

He bellowed at Claire, "Out, out my girl, get home at once!" Turning to O'Meara, he spluttered, "You wastrel," as he lifted what was left of O'Meara's dessert and shoved it into his face, making a right mess of his well-tailored suit and shirt.

Claire Scott was never seen in the Modena again. Shortly after that, she went to Trinity College, where she qualified as a doctor and emigrated to Canada. She was a real classy girl and later she married a prominent lawyer in Manitoba.

Those were the days when Killgriffin's young folk first learned the joys of eating out. Simple days when Faloona's café and the Modena were the culinary palaces of their youth, when wonderful Italian men like Luigi and Giovanni turned the town into a place of delight on dark, miserable nights.

Jim Brady

MY SON SUMIR

I have spent so many holidays in Kos that I grew to love the place and in 2005, the Mayor granted me honorary citizenship. During these years, I got to know two young guys, one Greek/Australian, one Indian/British, so well that they adopted me as their father calling me "Dad" in conversation. My having sons of different colours puzzled other holidaymakers, so I wrote this in explanation.

I remember the day well
It was the middle of the night
As the Patel family walked past
In the bright sunlight

All of a sudden came a stampeding
Tandoori elephant herd, one hundred or more,
And down on the Patel family
The whole lot bore

When they finally passed
And had flown off on their wings into the night
There in the road
Was a terrible sight

There stood Sumir
Unharmed all upset and afuddle
In the middle of what was now
A Patel puddle

I made him my son
On that sad day
And now my son Sumir
Forever he will stay

But some people say
"He is black and you're white"
Perhaps I was black
Before I got that fright

At the tandoori elephant stampede
On that day in the bright sunlight
That happened in India in the middle of the night

WHY THE WORLD IS ROUND

Dear Sir or Madam
With regards to your question
As to why the world is round

The reason is as follows:
If it were square, the people might trip
Over the corners and hurt themselves

But, you say, why not have oval?

Now that would be a bad mistake
For if it were oval
A hen might sit on it to hatch it
And smother all the people
The people on the top side

While all the people on the bottom
Would probably be killed by all the
Bodies falling down on top of them

Ria Duff

THE BARD

Extract from "Rell's Army"

With a small sigh, the Bard, Rell, leaned back in his chair until the front legs reared off the ground. He glanced out the window to the heavy rain thundering against the glass. The gale dragged the beads of rain in long, jagged tracks across the window pane. He was sure the harsh winds were ripping up trees in the forest beyond the castle grounds, but the ominous cracking was more likely to be a whiplash of thunder across the bulging skies.

He turned his attention back to the letter he had been struggling with. "Dear Majesty"; that was it. The right words for the king's letter were eluding him. Of course he knew what he wanted to write; it would be short, concise and honest, with no flowery flattery.

"Dear reader, I am writing because, as the rightful heir to the throne on which you sit, I feel it is my duty to inform you that you are running this kingdom into the ground. If you do not soon see fit to get off your royal arse and repeal the unjust laws you have forced on my people, the rebel leaders and myself will have no choice but to raze your palace to the ground and take back my grandfather's lands. You will find yourself hanged in the village square the following morning. Best wishes, Yours in good faith, the Bard."

Would the king appreciate his honesty? Rell didn't think so. Giving it up as a bad job, he rose and went to the window. He caught his reflection in the obsidian glass. Judging by the state of his hair, he may as well have been outside in the winds. His face was drawn and his eyes vacant under his thatch of unruly red curls. He was so tired. Maybe he would just skip the ball.

Oh Dagda! The ball. It was almost time. He had to make an appearance; as the head of the rebels, he must keep up his outward show with the Lords and Ladies. The Count and Countess of Arundel had been so kind to house the small band of fighters here; he couldn't repay them by missing their feast.

He turned slowly away from the window; nothing out there but the raging elements, sending the gardens into a flurry where a naked woman traipsed beneath the light from the castle windows.

Rell froze. He did not just see that! Did he? He looked again. Ah, of course. Only a dark sea of grass. He was imagining things. Not healthy, he thought. Still he didn't have time to worry. He glanced out the window – and swore. She was directly under the window now, looking straight up at him. Starkly white and shivering in the dark. Her arms crossed over her belly, rain streaming from her hair, down her face and shoulders. She gazed with haunted, searching eyes towards his window and spotted him. He met the pair of pale vortex eyes with a thrill of fright. For a long moment, he stared back at her, unable to look away from her tortured face.

The wind suddenly gave a dejected howl and Rell came to his senses. He snatched his cloak, hurtled down the spiral stairs towards the servants' doors, the most direct way onto the lawns. However when he reached the bottom and skidded across the grass to the place where the girl had been, there was only rain misted in the castle lights. He gasped, for she was now lying in a heap in the mud. The lighted windows illuminated the dark stream of blood trickling and splitting into streams along her back and flowing thick into the grass.

Rell stepped closer and saw that her body was curled and clenched in pain; in her right hand, she clutched an arrow, its tip still imbedded in the gored dark red flesh above her breast, no longer hidden by her tangle of hair. Rell quickly bundled up the cloak; the woman's modesty forgotten, he used it instead to try to stem the blood flow. He dared not attempt to remove the arrow, lest she bleed to death all the sooner. He carried her inside and yelled for someone to call the matron.

Maura McDonnell

SLOW TO KILL

The serpent
penetrated the womb
that bore me.
Tongue venomous
appetite insatiable.
A slow winding trail,
havoc and destruction
in its wake
a skeletal form,
my mother.
Months, weeks
excruciating pain —
scream — scream —
morphine —
a respite;
daily ablutions
shame in the eyes.
"You're my child now."
Journey ending
comatose —
eyes roll, lids flutter
a bird on the wing —
soaring — soaring —
gone.

| MY LOVE A STRANGER

Once more, I come.
Perhaps today
there may be some lucidity.
It's not to be.

My gentle giant
with the golden voice,
what do I see?

The once glossy black hair,
a mixture of white and grey tufts.
Twinkling brown eyes,
now – a vacant stare.
Hands that held mine,
clutching continuously
at the bedclothes.

Where are you my love?
In some strange world
wherein I cannot enter.

I call your name.
A spew of mutterings
my answer.
Silent tears
pull at my heartstrings.

Time to go.
Goodbye,
my strange love.

Oisín McGann

LOST FOR WORDS

It was around the time that the Spanish Armada was being tossed about on the seas off the west coast that Conn noticed he was beginning to miss words. He groaned and rubbed his eyes before looking at his watch. It was ten past two in the morning. He was on the second-last page of a five thousand-word essay on "ancient Irish seafaring" that was due in the following day – or rather, later that morning. And now he was missing words; he had left out the word "crest". He tipp-exed the end of the sentence and wrote it back in. When he read the sentence again, he found he had left out the last word, "rocks". He clicked his tongue and put it down.

It's funny though, he wondered, I could have sworn I had it down the first time. I must be more tired than I thought. He had been up since early the day before and the weariness lay like a lead blanket on his shoulders and across the back of his neck. His eyes felt puffy and every now and then his vision would blur so that he would have to blink to clear it.

Conn leaned back and stretched with all his might, groaning with the effort. He took a sip of lukewarm coffee and looked across at his notes, composing the next paragraph in his mind before putting pen to paper once more. The pen froze above the page. "Rocks", the last word he had written, was missing again. He frowned. He had definitely written it that time, he was positive. He screwed his eyes shut, pinched the bridge of his nose between finger and thumb and looked again. It was still gone.

He pushed himself back from the desk, as if distance would help. He stood up, walked to the door of the bedroom and back to the table again. No, he was just tired, that was all. What did he think? That the word had just off and disappeared? The fact that he was even thinking along those lines was proof enough that he was exhausted to the point of going bonkers. Maybe he should get a few hours' sleep. But Conn knew himself too well; once in bed he would not get up until at least late morning – it was far too easy when you were half asleep in a warm bed to think of perfectly good reasons for staying there. He was almost done, just another page and a half and he would be finished. Then he could sleep through the whole weekend if he wanted. It was bad enough he was not going to have time to type it, but he had to at least get it in before the deadline.

Conn sat down, picked up the pen and glanced at his notes. Pages of his neat, clear, joined-up hand-writing lay strewn across his desk. He must remember to get a new folder for all that stuff tomorrow. Conn liked folders; he liked the way they could make sloppy work look tidy and the way they made things easier to find. Everything looked organised when it was in a folder. His mind was wandering again; what did you call daydreaming when it happened at night? He stretched once more before writing "rocks" in again. He had got another two lines down when something moved in the corner of his vision. His gaze was drawn reflexively towards the spot in the text where the word "crest" had just been. He had never imagined that a five-letter word could leave such a big gap.

"Jesus!" he gasped.

He touched it with his fingers but the tipp-ex on the paper was bare. A closer check revealed the imprint that the pen had left, but no mark . . . no ink. He had seen himself write it, he had no doubt this time; he had seen that word in stark purple-black across the smooth white page.

Another movement caught his eye. There was a larger gap at the top of the page, on clean paper this time, where the word "Galway" had been. At this point, logic and common sense were flopping about like a fish in the bottom of a boat. Conn placed his hands on the desk and stared hard at the page.

His eyes bulged in disbelief as the word "anchors" unwound itself and wriggled towards the edge of the sheet. It made it to the margin, pushed itself over the edge and squirmed frantically like some thin, black worm in the direction of the shadows behind the desk-lamp.

Conn was not hampered by a lively imagination; he was instead blessed with a remarkably simple approach to life. A three-inch thick textbook slammed down on the inky fugitive. He lifted the book to see a squiggly biro mark on the desk, one that was not moving. With that sorted he got back to the business of meeting his deadline.

Even as he started to write, however, more words began to lift themselves from the paper, making a desperate bid for freedom. Conn scooped them back onto the paper, pushing them into their places, but he was fighting a losing battle. They would not form words again, writhing around and twisting under his fingers to defy his efforts to keep them in place. It was becoming impossible to stop them from getting away. Conn roared in frustration and swatted them with his hands but they wriggled between his fingers. He grabbed the textbook and flattened anything that moved, stamping on any that fell to the floor.

Eventually everything was still. He was breathing heavily and his skin was damp with sweat. He sat down and retrieved his pen from the floor. A scan of his desk told him that most of his notes and the larger part of his essay were still fairly intact. The page he had been working on was almost completely bare. Conn heaved a sigh and set about re-writing what had been lost. He was soon making progress, the flow of thought brought on by the rush of adrenaline. If he saw a word start to move, he squashed it flat again with the heavy book, developing a rhythm as time wore on: write with his right hand, slam with his left; write, slam, write, slam. It became quite natural after a while. Somebody in the flat above thumped on the ceiling, complaining about the racket, but Conn ignored them. End of term exams were at stake here.

But now the lines were squirming free even as they flowed from the ball-point. Some tried to slip away, others crawled up the length of the pen, twisting around it only to be crushed beneath his fingers. Like eels, they wiggled elusively, refusing to be kept down. Conn stood up and leaned down as hard as he dared on the biro, impaling the words onto the page. He was sweating heavily now, the frustration taking its toll. This had to stop, he could not take much more. It was then that he spied movement on some of the other pages, there was a rustling sound like a thousand insects shuffling their feet. There was no time – he was going to lose everything. He wrenched one of the desk drawers open and rooted through the jumble of contents, there was only one thing he could do now . . .

University College Dublin was the usual beehive of toing and froing that Thursday morning; students walking among the cold concrete buildings, standing out on the grass or by the lake, chatting, or cycling on the thoroughfares. Baggy combat trousers and trainers, the mainstay of college fashion, were this season complemented by tousled heads, indie band T-shirts, hoodies and body-piercings in every piece of anatomy accessible by needle. Everyone had bags of books, easy smiles and the carefree attitude that even the threat of assessments and exams could not yet darken.

It was a pale and drawn Conn McAllister that shuffled wearily towards the history department that morning. There were bruise-dark bags under his eyes and an astute observer would have noted the tight hold he kept on the folder underneath his right arm.

He stuck his head around the door of the history professor's office, waved the essay vaguely and placed it on her desk.

"Thank you, Conn, late night was it?" she asked.

"Very late, yes," he replied in a cracked voice.

He went to leave. The professor glanced at the pages and frowned.

"Conn?"

He turned back, raising his eyebrows as if it was the only way he could keep his eyes open. The lecturer held up the sheets:

"Why did you laminate them?"

Amy L Hibbitts

WORDS TO A SOLDIER

They die because they're different,
They die because they're young,
They die because they're old
But never for what they've done.

Shoot them because you're told to,
Shoot them because you can,
Shoot them because they hate you
But it won't make you a man.

Laugh because you are happy,
Laugh because you have won,
Laugh because you think it's over
But it's only just begun.

So cry because you're sorry,
Cry because you can't scream,
Cry for as long as you want, but
You'll never wake up from this dream.

| BORDERS

This land was once quiet
Until they came,
Dividing our people
Feeling no fear or shame
Now blood is spilt in street and lane.

With guns in our hands
And no guilt in their heart
Turning our land to ruins
Wrenching our people apart.

Though talk we might
There is no change,
Merely takes up our time
And redefines the range.

Living our lives by opinions
That were never our own,
But bred into us from birth
With that proud, defiant tone.

Never could we play
With the boy down the street,
For 'though outside he was the same
He was different underneath.

And 'though try hard we might
Will it ever be done?
Can we finish the war
Our grandfathers had begun?

But with metal in my heart
And a gun in my cold hand,
Peace is not something
I can ever understand.

Bridie Clarke

OUT OF TUNE

When I get time
I'll plant a tree
Make gooseberry jam
Walk the dog and not rush
Read a book by the fire
Be more patient and kind
When I get time . . .

When I get time
I'll play with you child
Maybe go to the Zoo
We'll walk on the beach
Throw stones in the sea
Or we'll just sit and chat
When I get time . . .

When I get time
I'll smile at the sun
And laugh in the rain
Stop yapping so much
And listen more often
I'll dance on my toes
And sing out of tune
When I get time . . .

When I get time
If I had time
I *never* have time
But from now on
I'm *taking* the time
And *making* the time
While I still have time . . .

44

Lillie Callan

SENIOR CITIZEN

Recently I was asked what it was like to be a senior citizen or, in other words, what it was like to be an old age pensioner. After a bit of thought I said, "It's wonderful. I am my own boss, I can go to bed and get up when I like and I can enjoy my family and my grandchildren. It is just great."

Or so I thought until I met Jack McGrath at the Post Office and I mentioned that a girl from the local paper was writing a piece about senior citizens and had interviewed me. I told him what I'd said.

Well, two and half hours later I returned home deflated, depressed, a headache; you name it: I had it.

He had wedged me up against the Post Office door. Said he, "What are you talking about? When I come into the town now, it's impossible to get a bit of plain, ordinary grub like cabbage and bacon or a cup of tea and a bun. Last week," said he, "I went into one of those places with marble floors, walls and tables – it was like a hospital clinic – and over comes a young waitress and she shone like wax.

"'Well, sir,' said she, 'can I help you?'

"'Indeed you can,' I said. 'Get me a pot of tea and a bun.'

"'Would you like camomile, thyme, sage–?'

"'Stop, stop,' said I. 'Put a teabag in a mug and put boiling water on it.' It was the same procedure about the bun. I brought a flask with me today," said he.

"God be with the time," he said, "when I went over to Kate in the Post Office and there'd be about ten of us there on a Friday morning and Kate would make the tea for us and have currant bread. I wouldn't have to buy a paper then. I'd have all the news and happenings of the parish. It was a real community sitting around Kate's fire."

I thought he'd finished and I could move on but he didn't stop there. "If you have to go to the doctor now," said he, "you have to wait three or four hours. In the old days, you only had to mention a pain or an ache and Lizzie Maguire would have a cure. Bread soda for the heartburn. Mustard seed for the chest. Josie Daly had a garden of weeds and there was a cure in every one of them."

Again I tried to make my getaway but he said, "Will you ever forget the missions, the smell of sweat, porter and tobacco all rolled into one? Now they want beautiful bodies, washing all the oil out of them and the houses are mansions. In our time, it was two or three rooms and ten children; now it's ten rooms and two children. They have toilets in every room. They even have one at the back door."

He turned around real quick and, with a sour tone, he said, "How could you say these are great times, when you can't leave your house without locking doors and windows or it will be cleaned out before you get home. You have to put your few euro in the bank and you can't understand a word the young people are talking about in them places. There's nobody in the mansions; they're all working to keep them. There's nobody about during the day and, if you do see anybody, you immediately think they're going to rob you."

I said I had to catch a bus but I might as well have said I had to catch a corncrake. He moved after me with a hold of my arm and he said, "Will you ever forget the dances? I could jive and dance like Fred Astaire. I was never short of a partner. The women were on one side and the lads on the other. I would look up and down the line and make a beeline for my woman.

"Near the end of the night, you would ask her if she would like a mineral and, if she accepted, you knew you were right for the night." Said he, "You would always be hoping she lived fairly close as I hadn't even a bicycle. There would be a lot of whispering and nibbling but no main course until after the wedding."

I just had enough and I said, "Jack, those were the days when men were men and women had to put up with a lot and, thank God, the wheel has turned and we are equal."

I put my head in the air and I thought, "His glass is half empty but my glass is almost full."

Ciaran Hodgers

WHILE DRIFTING TO SLEEP

Sometimes night,
Isn't always so still
When insomnia flows like caffeine through your veins.
When you await a prayer replied
Or when the tears you know haven't been shed . . .
Yet . . .
Still ripple softly in your brain.
Sometimes night,
Isn't always so quiet
People's internal shouting here and there again
As the spiders dressed in despair
Each convulsive syllable; ball on chain . . .
Bound...
Decide their usual visit.

Sometimes night,
Isn't always so dark,
With heaven dancing behind the brown in your eyes,
Or the breath your touch creates.
How dark above, the clouds may counsel to . . .
Rain . . .
Their tyranny shall not exhaust.

DANCE FOR DEATH, |
FEAST FOR REBIRTH |

Listen to the drumming,
a rhythmic beat.
Hear it humming,
beneath your feet.

Watch the dancing,
thrice abound.
See the magick,
all around.

Sense the old one,
O Horned God.
Feel it be done.
Chalice and rod.

This is Lughnasadh,
the mighty death.
This is Wicca,
the divine rebirth.

Plants may die,
and Yule may come.
Do not try,
it must be done.

This is the vision,
wheel of the year.
This is religion,
release your fear.

Brian Quinn
THIS TABLE

This table,
These spoons,
The empty coffee cups,
The unused sugar sachets,
The crowded café,
This person loved
And was loved

This table,
Those hands,
The stains on the saucer,
The crumpled napkin,
The multitudinous conversations,
Crumbs of comfort
Littering the table

This table,
That voice,
The soft tinted hair,
The proud nose,
The eyes darting and delving,
Overlapping lives
Now unfolded and separated

This table,
This room,
That person,
That body,
The sharp intellect,
Is over there,
Somewhere.

THE EMBRACE |

Body heat
Fills vacant spaces
As alternate shapes
Slide into opposing contours
Capturing the affection
Holding brings,
Warmth rises
In the heaving closeness
While breathing slows
Encircled in comfort
And rhythm,
A resting head
Listens
To a beating heart
Arms fill
With touch and feeling
And clinging
Has never felt so complete
Or so empty
When the embrace slips,
Cracks and breaks apart,
Hands try
To linger and hold,
Their last touch
That slides
And reluctantly
Lets go.

| YOUTH

Petulance is annoying
In someone so young,
Especially when your references
For experience
Are snotty noses
Water paints, magic crayons
And school-yard
Psychology.
Your boundless enthusiasm
And energy
Is grating and insulting,
When disregarding
An attained struggle
For knowledge and wisdom.
Yet you stride through obstacles
With the vision and care
Of an old man
Born as a youth.
Your calm temperament
Is disturbing,
Your passion
For dreams and desires
Is frankly
Infuriating,
And your loyalty
Can only be returned
With daggers, smiles,
And an earned unworthiness.

Shannon Walsh

SHOT

no crack, no bang,
no dramatic turn
but still i fell.
blood flowing,
but joy
knowing that
soon i'd leave that place.
morphine pumping,
pain numbing,
pretty nurse's face.

Maggie Pinder

THE DAY GEORGE BEST DIED

The day George Best died was bitter. A cutting wind swept down from the north, slicing through brick and bone alike. The slatey sea from England fused into the sky and the horizon was filled with ghosts. Ailsa checked the oil gauge, winced, turned the heating on anyway.

The papers were calling him dead even though he wasn't. Maybe not alive and kicking, but alive, hobbling along, on a ventilator, conscious, lying wooden in a coma, aware, sedated. If he'd been shown the papers that day, would he have died early to appease their headline writers?

Ailsa's car wouldn't start. The little Ford turned over once and refused to oblige again. Gerard had the other car, the bigger car, the faster car, the real car, not this little matchbox with a broken aerial and keyed paint. Nought to sixty in sixty minutes.

The day George Best died, Gerard wasn't home. He'd stayed in Dublin the night before, citing late hours, a business dinner, the traffic, although the M1 would be empty that late at night. He'd stayed over in a business expense hotel room on St Stephen's Green.

George Best's wife wasn't allowed to see him either.

It was four miles to the shops, along a tiny lane that wound around the coast. With no car, she could walk it in an hour if she left the kids behind, locked in the house. She was a good mother; she'd remove sharp objects and matches. Or she could drag along the whining toddler and the baby and it would take two.

The day George Best died, her oldest son came home from school, shouting for his football kit.

"Where are my boots?" he screamed. "I know I left them in the hallway."

Ailsa yelled back about respect, about not being his bloody slave, and about how it was a wonder he found his head in that pigsty he called his room. Aidan screamed that George Best had women to wash his kit and return it Persil-white and folded on the foot of his bed.

"Fine," she said, "You move out and find some poor fool to do that for you."

Aidan stormed out, and she found twenty euro missing from her purse.

The day George Best died was the day of the final demand for the phone bill. Gerard earned enough, but where was it all?

"I spent a fortune on booze, birds and fast cars. And I squandered the rest," said George Best.

Ailsa poured a cream sherry, swallowed it in one gulp, filled the glass again. Cooking sherry didn't count; it's not like it were whiskey. George Best was the one with the thirst for the drink, not her. She'd make veal with sherry and mushroom sauce for dinner, that would use up the bit that was left in the bottle, and then she'd buy another one. The veal was Gerard's favourite, she'd make it for him, as a surprise.

The day that George Best died was the day it fell apart.

Ah, for a life like George Best.

THE 5:15 TO WOLVERHAMPTON

On the 5:15 train to Wolverhampton, Ginevra tells Dinesh she is leaving him.

Dinesh stares at her in bewilderment. "But why? I thought we were happy."

Ginevra shrugs and her gaze moves to the window. Outside, the rows of terrace houses slide into the darkness.

"Are you going to tell me why?"

"Does it matter? It's not important."

"It matters to me." Disbelief gives way to anger, fuelled by her indifference. The hurt sits in his stomach like the solid rye bread she loves so well, heavy and indigestible.

The weight of words she won't say stretches between them. It's an uneasy moment, overlaid with her indifference. The train clatters on, gathering speed, and the lights of the houses flash past. Other people live in those houses, thinks Dinesh. Happy people, with families. Having dinner, yelling at their kids, mopping up their dhal with chunks of naan bread, sitting peaceably in front of the telly.

The carriage sways. He looks at her, pale and remote in the dim light. Around them, commuters unfurl *The Guardian*, text their partners to meet them at the station.

"Is it because I'm Indian?" he asks.

She transfers her gaze to him, and there's a tender amusement in her face. "Don't be silly."

The softness he sees makes him think he can mend this, bridge the gap between them, glue them back together, but her next words shatter that illusion.

"There's someone else."

He swallows, carefully. Pride keeps his voice steady, and he asks, "Do I know him?"

"Her. And no, you don't."

Slow, steady breaths. Don't let her see his incomprehension; don't let her see his instinctive recoil. He reaches between them, clasps her hand.

"I'm happy for you."

"Truly?" Her face glows, and the words tumble out to fill the gulf he'd never realised was there. "Oh, Dinesh, you must meet her. She's amazing, everything I've ever looked for. It's never been like this before, not for me."

He listens to her prattle, and the walls build themselves, brick by brick, around his heart. He studies their intertwined hands, soft white skin to caramel brown skin.

If his heart weren't breaking, he would laugh at his own stupidity.

John Doherty

THE PIG

One day I was looking into a field
At a pig that was grazing there
When a farmer came along and said
"With him, none can compare.

"That pig is a walking genius
There's nothing he cannot do
He dragged the doctor to the house
When I had a dose of flu.

"One dark night last winter
Thieves attempted to rob my farm
He quickly got into his stride
And set off the burglar alarm.

"My granny fell down the stairs
Once when all alone
He managed to call the ambulance
By grunting into the phone.

"Then there was the incident
The hay, it went on fire
He rescued all the cattle
By opening up the byre.

"And on another occasion
Two sheep fell down a hole
He was able to rescue them
By climbing down a pole."

The farmer said, "He can do many tricks
At a command he sits and begs."
And while he was demonstrating this
I saw he had only three legs.

"I see he has lost a leg," I cried,
"No doubt in some courageous act
Attempting a daring rescue
Or keeping someone's life intact."

"Not really," said the farmer.
He stooped and tickled his head.
"I'll tell you about the leg now
And then he goes to bed.

"Beside him the cleverest animal
Would look like a stupid dunce
So when you get a brilliant pig like this
You don't eat him all at once."

| THE PHONE CALL

Recently, I went to bed
Feeling extremely tired
Having endured a stressful day
In fact I had been fired

The telephone started ringing
I hate those calls at night
You expect it's bad news
And sometimes you are right

An angry male was on the line
He was shouting and upset
Clearly very much disturbed
His voice I can't forget

"My wife is having an affair
I believe it is with you
And I want to let you know
This is something you will rue.

"That you should even try
To tear my marriage asunder
Means you are going to find out
You've made the biggest blunder.

"My feeling is you'll deny events
For I think you're cowardly too
I cannot see how my wife
Could ever take to you.

"Our lives were going smoothly
'Til you came on the scene
Without a thought for decency
You really are obscene.

"Be man enough and admit it
You spineless little rat."
He was beside himself with rage
I was plainly aware of that.

"I want a straightforward answer
Have you been seeing my wife?
A person who behaves like that
Is the lowest form of life."

I said, "I'd like to co-operate
And give the info you are seeking
But before I can be of any help
Please tell me who is speaking."

AMERGIN AWARDS
2005
WINNER:
JUNIOR SHORT STORY

Bronagh Gaynor

(AGE 11)

THE ESCAPE

It was Monday morning in Rockwood School in the town of Bullberry. Usually at 9.30 a.m. the class would do spellings and tables, but, today was not an ordinary day. It was very different because they were doing a Maths and History test. Everyone hated these subjects and not a single person had done any revision. A while before the test started, Ms Byrne asked if anyone would like to go to the toilet. Nicole was so nervous that her hands started to sweat, so she went to the toilet to wash her hands. When she was finished, she quickly grabbed a tissue and then, just out of the corner of her eye, she spotted a small hole in the middle of the wall. As soon as she saw it, a brilliant idea popped into her head. "We are going to escape!"

So, on 11th February 2005 at 10.00 a.m., the work began. Throughout the morning, girls were going in and out to the toilet with a ruler or pen hidden in their pockets for scraping and poking at the hole in the wall. Things were moving very well, it was getting bigger and bigger by the minute. So far around twelve girls had gone to the bathroom and five still had to go before the break, which was just before the exams were about to start. But time was catching up on us and, at a quarter to eleven, the school bell rang for break time. This was when we were going to make our move.

As soon as our teacher – Ms Byrne – left the room, we all made a run for it. One by one, each of us went into the bathroom and carefully crawled into the large hole in the wall. As the last girl stood at the door, waiting her turn to go in, she could hear the sound of Ms Byrne's high heels clip-clopping across the path coming closer and closer. The long line of children moved quickly and, by the time she reached the door, everyone was safe and sound inside the hole and well away from those dreaded tests. All of a sudden the bell rang for the end of the break. Children from Ms Burke's class, Mrs Bell's class and Ms Wood's class were all standing quietly in their lines, but, alas!, there were no fifth- and sixth-class pupils to be seen.

Ms Byrne stepped out of her classroom like she always did – she was wearing high heels, a long black coat and she had a cup of hot water with a slice of lemon in it in her hand. She had a huge smile on her face – she couldn't wait to get started with the exams. But, as soon as she realised we were not there, the smile went and a huge shocked expression appeared on her face.

"No! No! No!" she roared.

Ms Byrne could not believe her girls were missing. Normally we were the first class to line up at the end of the break, but not a single eleven- or twelve-year-old pupil could be seen anywhere.

It was fantastic – we just couldn't believe we had done it. By twelve noon we were still crawling down the hole. It was dark, cold, wet and scary but nobody really cared as long as we were far away from those dreaded exams.

Ms Byrne was panicking so much that she couldn't even stand on her own two legs, because there was not much time left of school and she needed to find her pupils quickly. But we definitely were not turning back.

We eventually arrived at the end of the tunnel. There were three different paths and we were not sure which way we should go. In the end we picked the one on the left side and away we all set off. At the end of the path luckily there was a ladder and one by one we climbed up and what we saw made us all gleam with delight. We were at a Sweet Shop but not just any Sweet Shop – it was one of the biggest Sweet Shops in town. The last of the girls didn't walk up the ladder, they ran! We ate so much that some of the girls were starting to feel sick.

As for poor Ms Byrne, she had a bad panic attack – she just couldn't handle the strain of not finding her pupils that day. She spent the next few weeks sitting at home, all alone with her test papers and not a single question answered. As for us, the clever and brave pupils, we were fine. We had a substitute teacher who, like us, wasn't too fond of Maths and History herself. The hole is now closed up but that's not going to stop us escaping again!

AMERGIN AWARDS
2005
WINNER:
JUNIOR POETRY

Niamh McGuinness

(AGE 15)

THE MAN OF SHINING SONG

A street roaring with the din of clamouring human life
Full to bursting with people, son, daughter, husband, wife
Gaudy neon signs compete unnecessarily for my interested glance
These eyes are blind to it all, the background pales. I've been
entranced.

By something not quite in keeping with the rowdy scene
Not loud, brash, noisy or overly keen
In grabbing any attention, it bellows no rousing call
It's the solitary figure of a Dublin busker, oblivious to all.

He cradles his guitar as one would a precious new-born child
This gentility conflicts with an appearance so wild
His cheeks unshaven, his clothes in graceful tatters
He carries on regardless, it's the music that matters.

His unruly dark head bent low, his eyes are shut tight
Yet nobody notices that he is singing with all of his might
The notes are vivid, swimming lazily
Toward me. I can almost see them, shining hazily.

Such a beautiful gift to share with people on this street
Who wear the cobbles down, trudging along with weary feet
I drop a coin into a polystyrene cup, to the empty bottom I watch it
sink
He stops playing, acknowledging this rarity with a grateful wink.

Arthur Sheridan

SPIDER

AMERGIN AWARDS
2005
WINNER:
ADULT SHORT STORY

It flows. Pushed on by the fluid. Rushing through my system. Like grains of sand. Through an hour glass. Numbing. Sands of time tickling. Causing itches then scratching them. I shift my position. The grains of silver tilt within me. Ecstasy reverberates from, then flows back into them. The ceiling's grey and flowing. Egg shelled paint curling. Crispy. Gaping at me, then accepting me.

"Ann. Ann." Ann. The name I hate. My name. Practical. Purely functional. No frills. No letters wasted. Dull. Then again, everybody hates their name. Don't they?

"Ann." He calls in his old voice. In this house of old. Old house. Old people. Old smells. Dark old, sad old. Old and cranky. Too old to be a parent. Then again, he's not my parent.

The spider swings and spindles. Dangling, swinging, jumping, frolicking. On liquid crystal gossamer. Climbing and swinging from the curling paint crisp, where he sleeps, to the light flex. Building a fine mesh. Happily swinging.

"Ann." He cries for me to come. His weak croaky old voice. Why call me now? Now that I was content with my cloud mattress buzzing under my bum. An unhappy man. A miserable man. A man that always needed looking after. Not a man for tact. Oh no. "We're not your real parents," he said. My heart dropped through my stomach and thumped my seat. Flossie made faces at him to shut his mouth, but oh no. He had to tell. I was dazed. I floated on a sick sea. Their voices distant like background noise. Yet clear like speaking through a mesh filter. A thumping in my chest. Pumping.

"Yiz are liars, liars," I thought. A cruel joke. A trick. Fourteen is too old to be told. Too old.

"Eleven kids. They couldn't look after them all, so they gave you to us," Flossie explained. Kind Flossie. Flossies couldn't have kids. He looked pained at her kindness. He always looked pained. Like a wounded animal. Jealous of others' comfort. Always ready to inflict pain himself. They'd given me away. Me. Away. To whom? To these people. Old people. Drunk old people. Always time for another one. Never pass a pub. They couldn't have known. My real parents couldn't have known. They wouldn't have left me with these people. Not these people. Playing outside the pub. Years of it. How many oranges and packets of crisps can you eat anyway? I can smell the soul of pubs. Brown pubs. Brown air. Brown stained hands. Brown smell, Guinness sweat and nicotine, rising off everything. Floor. Furniture. Bar. Walls. Clothes. People. People glad to see me.

"Ah she's a lovely girl. Sit on me knee. Oh she's getting very tall." Whiskey breath. Porter breath. Red nose. Old hands. Yellow wrinkled hands. Brown stained hands. Touching, feeling, creeping, seeking. Escape to the toilets. Wet toilets. Wet floor, damp air, Dettol smell. Dark, grey, peeling, curling. No refuge here. Into the noise again. Faces through a smoke cloud. Yellow smiles. The noise of laughter and spittle. Gaping mouths. Yellow teeth. The stagger. The swaying. The slowing, of movement and time. The time warp of drunk. The laughter so easily turning to anger. Simmering. Waiting for an excuse to escape. A joke not laughed at. A hero put down. I grab my coat. Make my way to the door away from molesting eyes. To the dull grey light outside. My saviour is in my pocket. Grey. Balding. Thread bare. But still with plenty of bounce. Tennis balls are best. Even if old.

"Where you going, Bob? Down the lane, Bob? For what, Bob?" Grunts. Garbled anger down the lane. He sits there in his wet. Exposed flattened phallus. Yellow, wrinkled. Swinging his arm. Cigarette stub in brown fingers aimed for his greying capped head. Sometimes content grunts. Sometimes angry. Mostly content in his lapping wee. Alcohol's happiness. But it would wear off. Then someone would feel the brunt of his anger. Or maybe he would turn it inward on himself. Mind drifting with the movement of the balls.

"For Rhubarb." Safe in my escape but they would not work forever.

"Ann. Ann." The buzzing fading. Leaving. Going, going, almost gone.

"Ann." His voice weaker. Hoarser. Silver grains to sugar. Dissolving. Fluid slowing. Pump failing. Dangling spider retreats to curling paint. Better go to him. Maybe he'll know. My eyes. He's always suspicious. He knows something. Probably checked his pockets, knows he's short.

"You spent it in the bookies," I'll say. He was drunk. "Do you not remember?" Ha ha. Try to lift myself from the mattress. Comfortable. Body doesn't want to go. Why call me now? So little comfort in life. Try to detach myself from this feeling of effort my body's going through. I turn on to autopilot. My body is light. Movement is slow. Like dance. Ballet. Deliberate. I drift down the stairs. Graceful. Light. I'm a floating feather. Getting closer. His voice clearer. The door ajar. That smell. Dirty smell. He looks up. Glad to see me. Smell of fear. Me his comforts. His strength. I can see it in his eyes. So clearly. I'm surprised.

"Are you alright?"

"Ann, Ann. Thank God."

"I'll call an ambulance."

"No. Don't go. Not yet. Wait." He's so frightened. Weakened. Grey face. Small face. Strength now only in his eyes, silvering eyes. I kneel beside him. His hands grab mine. White wrinkled hands. Sweat dampened. Cold. He's so glad to see me. He needs me. He loves me. I'm his little girl.

"I have to tell you." And I love you too, daddy.

"It wasn't me. I didn't want to. I told her not to. But she wanted a child so much. It was only to be for a little while. But she couldn't let go." I loosened my grip. His tightens.

"Everyday she got more attached. So she sent out feelers and you responded. And settled. When they settled in London they came back for you. But you wouldn't go. You screamed the house down. I told her it was wrong."

He tells me about my parents. Where they live now. What good. He grips my hand tighter. Looking for acceptance. For forgiveness. And I hold his hand, just looking at him. Not anymore loosening or tightening my grip. Listening as the whole sorry mess pours out. His body hardening but his soul never softer. Confessing. Looking for love. But still not giving. And I love you too, daddy. Love. Poxy love. Love is for poxers. Stuff love. And he reveals the whole sorry story. Word for sorry rotten word.

"I better get that ambulance now."

"No. Don't go." The silver in his eyes dulling.

"You'll be alright. I won't be a minute. I'll send Mary in while I'm phoning." Turning towards the door. I hear him plead for the first time ever.

"I want you Ann. Don't go." Ah, you'll be alright. I went next door to Mary's. She rushed in at the news. I stood dialling. The man at the other end seemed routine and unhurried, asking which service. In another time warp. The time warp of calm.

Mary stands over the body.

"He was just going as I came in." The fucker was telling the truth.

"The ambulance will be here in a minute." The ambulance, the police, the coroner, the social worker. The questions. Still four years 'til eighteen. Put in care. I haven't the time for this. I have a quest. I remember the address, he said. I empty his pockets for something to remember him by. The cash smiles back at me.

I feel the bumps and rhythms float through me chasing away my sleep. Only five hours 'til London. Dust and cigarette ash and cold. Not like the ads. Expressway me arse. The address he said imprinted in my brain. I drift in and out of sleep brought on by loneliness. Faces sitting apart. All sad. All lonely. All the lonely. Where do they all come from? My stomach is acid and empty. Mouth dry. Throat sore. Exhaustion overcomes discomfort. I drift. I dream. I see him on the floor. His eyes fishlike. Inanimate. His mouth gaping. No movement. But his soul egging me on. And then Flossie comes to me. Hugging me. Loving me. Warm feeling. Warm to warning. Trying to stop me. Controlling me. Telling me to turn back. Doom and gloom. Flossie the bastard. And then there they are. My real parents. Clean. Articulate. Younger than Flossie and him. Loving me. Caring for me. Oozing goodness. I hear voices. Hard uncaring voices. They don't match.

"You're here, missie. Last stop. We have to clean the carriage." I wake. In shock. Stunned. Noise. Train station noise. I'm shivering. Cold. My head hurts. I see a face. An old face. Cigarette in mouth. Irritated. Impatient at my sluggishness.

"We have to clean the carriages." I rise. Dazed. Go into the noise. Confused. People everywhere. The sun is well up. Must be about eleven. Where do I go? Which way do I turn? Bumping. Bustling. Must find a way out. A taxi. Find a taxi. He'll know the way. He'll deliver me. Deliver us from evil.

The house is big. Old. Worn. Dumpy looking. Still.

"Hello I'm looking for . . ."

He listened patiently, expectantly.

"You just missed them love. They've just left for the church. You got the letter then. Which one are you?"

I made the church. And everything else. Sick dream. Sick world. My heart lowered with the coffin. I kicked in some clay. Two days. I'd missed her by two days. She was the last. He'd gone two years earlier. The others were there. All ten. Back to the pub. Porter smell. Brown air. The others didn't seem bothered much. Drinking. Laughing. Telling stories. Telling lies. Terrible terrible lies. I got up and ran. Ran and ran and ran. I look at the landlady. She looks at me.

"No suitcase." I nod, trying to look away from the enquiring eyes. Suspicious eyes. Suspicion turns to greed. But I don't care. I pay anyway. And rush up the unlit stairs. Into the unlit room. Away from the eyes. Away from the lies. Anywhere will do. Just soon. Quick. The light brightens the emulsion over wallpaper. Old pattern. Old paint. Paint curling on moulding ceiling. Bulb hanging from bare flex. Miserable. The mix dissolves on the spoon. Soon. Quick. Lying bastards.

"Drunks. Both of them. Dried out regulars. Each of us taken into care. One by one." Scum. Mix in, air out. Shove in. Suck in. My stomach tingles at the thought. Soon. Rest. The pumping starts. The grains form and flow. I drift and pump and rush. The grains rush with the fluid. Vibrating, oscillating, reverberating. Their essence flowing out beyond the veins, beyond me. Filling the room. This is stronger than I'm used to at home. My cloud lifts up. Rotating. Spinning. Spinning out of myself. Ever upwards. Up to heaven. Up to the ceiling. And I lie safe behind the curling paint. And dream of spindling.

AMERGIN AWARDS
2005
WINNER:
ADULT POETRY

Barbara Flaherty

DARK RAVEN

Upon the death of my mother

Today the hare hides beneath
the fallen tree. Deep leaves
linger on the bare blades
of grass, fingers faded made
cold, cawing like a warning,
a chill come hard like mourning.
A daughter hides inside
a tearless cry. Mother died.
That blackbird heard. How many
memories blur into any
sense – sound of blue black bird
found, eyed high, heard, can stir,
can touch my hair tangled in
the root of you. Old tree, broken
branch of my branch. A small twig
is croaking a click clicking
click down in broken throated
sounds. Seed of your soil, spouted
flower and fruit of your ground,
no tears found, river underground
dried, died. Only click click sounds
in the nave of my voice pound
like heart beats pulsing in a cave.
A dark raven prayed today.

Brian Langan |
STILL LIFE |

I

The scene is set:
a vase, opaque, opalescent,
reflective of earth symmetry;
to the side, brilliant vermillion casts
a bold sward of contrast set
against the centre – a bowl,
golden apples, balls of sunlight.
The light of open window breezes
consolidating simple objects
in their awkward, balanced, unnatural poise.

II

Your unbound eye unites them in focus;
synapses fuse image to retina, essence to surface;
you see the parts made whole;
mind's eye fixes;
you breathe in calm solace;
practised hand dips brush in paint
– a beat, brief uncertainty –
then you begin.

III

I speak vainly to the you inside you –
like visiting a tomb with no death-date.
Your features are graven letters,
dulled eyes stilled of recognition.
This frame a husk, voiceless, memory-less replica;
yet the still soul of a life remains.
Brief synapse flares:
memory of luminescence;
a sudden hand jerks up and across,

68

remembering brushstrokes,
before the still life settles again
to the trapped beauty within.

IV

The painting hangs, *memento mori,*
its frame a cruel delimiter.
Within, lustrous restless energy,
more real than simple objects placed:
the kernel of the thing itself –
the vase, the bowl, the cloth,
and apple's juicy memory.

| NOAH'S DILEMMA

Two by two, he said.
For the life of me,
We'll never get them all aboard.
Ten dozen different breeds of cow;
Hundreds of cats and dogs;
Three hundred and fifty thousand
Species of beetle!
Wood lice!!
And bacteria? Diphtheria? Typhoid?!
Fuck it
Scuttle her
We're going down.

FENCEPOSTS |

Two old friends lean on the bar
"Evenin' Micka"
"Ah, howya Johnser,
How's she cuttin'?"
"Aaahhhhh ———"
"Can I get you—"
"The usual, good man."
"Two pints then."

They look at the view in the bar's mirror
Same view as yesterday, same last year.
The Norman keep overgrown with generations on generations.
The field where battles echoed now grazed and dozed
by Micka's son-in-law

"Grand evenin'"
"'Tis, 'tis . . . aye."

Micka is a gentleman farmer of the mind
Dirt poor, but not so's you'd notice.
The height of Frankenstein's monster,
A bolt through his bull-thick neck completes the effect;
The ragged stubble wire-wool scratches the collar.
Thinning beard now a shock of white
To balance his dung-brown mane.
He stands straight a moment,
Clears his throat, thinks better of it,
Hitches braced trousers high,
Crosses and recrosses his arms
And leans back on the bar
The polished mahogany worn
From his decades of sweat.

Johnser is . . .
Johnser's a sorry sight
He squints in the smoky light

This is his natural habitat, the limit of his view.
He scratches his liver-spotted pate,
The few strands remaining dancing away from his fingers.
His sharp forehead shadows a sickly pallor, as they used to say.
Something is encrusted on the sleeve of his jacket.
He hawks and spits to the side, not looking.
Bangs his pipe, and starts again.

The long wait ends:
Two frothing pillars of night
Rise up and leave milk moustaches.
The chorus: "Aaahhhh . . ."
"Grand shtuff," pronounces Micka
"Aye . . ."

Claudia Terry

COMFORTABLY NUMB
Extract from "The Anchorous Sea"

As a child she saw the world differently, as all children do. Now she hears whispers of her younger self. Yesterday, when the house was empty of her children, children who never whisper, she paused briefly in the arch separating kitchen and sitting room. With the alert ears of a young mother, instinctive and feline, she drops back on slippered heels and waits for the sound to come again. When it does come, she simply draws her dressing gown nearer, anticipating the sigh of wind that will end the whispers. The kettle shrieks, beckoning her into the present and she continues on into the kitchen and the ritual of her day.

Seated with coffee (that her sister tells her not to drink because her sister's doctor believes that it promotes the growth of tumours), she reflects on the elusive sound. It comes again and she recognises it – the flutter of clothes air-drying on a windy day, a breeze whistling though the mesh screens (that he put on the windows to keep the house cool and the insects out), the dancing of onion peels on the dirty kitchen floor (she meant to throw them out yesterday). It is not the individual sounds that she knows but the orchestral combination of all and the wind that conducts it. She sits quietly for a long time, anticipating the sound and relishing the feeling that it brings.

Her mother kept the onions and the eggs in one basket on the windowsill. His mother despaired at her doing this and now she keeps the eggs in the fridge. A wire chicken half-filled with onions sits on the sill. She is not like her mother. Her mother would not change her way to please another. She kept her name and her eggs and her way of living intact throughout her life and lived comfortably and knowingly beside what was expected.

The phone rings. "Just checking if you're alright," he asks.

"Yes," she answers, and hopes that this one word will be enough to begin and end the conversation.

"What are you doing? Are you still in bed?"

"Yes."

"You should get up, have a coffee, a shower."

"I will," she replies, to end the conversation, realising that "yes" will not do.

"Good. I'll call later. Take care of yourself, Zottie. 'Bye now."

He has used a nickname that was once endearing but now seems out of context. She turns off the phone.

Cataclysm *n.* violent break, disruption.

Numb *a. & v.t.* deprived of feeling or power of motion.

When he'd asked her to think of words to identify herself, she could only think of two words: "cataclysm" and "numb". Pink Floyd had been a favourite. Back then she'd listened to *Comfortably Numb*, hearing the music and knowing the words but they did not yet ring in her head like a mantra. Later, the peculiar word combination haunted her. Lying in the dark, wrapped tight in a feather duvet trying to stop her heart from beating by holding her breath . . . she knew the possibilities that "comfortably numb" was. But her heart was strong and the duvet always fell free in the morning's light.

He said that "numb" was not surprising. "It is common to feel numb when one has been through such an ordeal." (**Ordeal** *n.* an experience that tests character or endurance, severe trial).

She felt that "numb" was a place somewhere deep in the centre of her being. It was a place she might wish herself, often or not, but she always had it and she felt it like a shiver down her spine. It was a void where she might forget to feel or a hollow, echoing dark place that was somehow comforting like the smell of wet dog. Numb was not a conclusion, as she felt his words implied.

"Tell me about 'cataclysm'," he asks, pronouncing the word as a Latin scholar might.

"Which one?" she challenges.

"Why do you identify with this word?"

"Doesn't it sound grand?" she tries to be funny but he remains straight-faced and expectant of her answer. "Maybe I meant 'cataclysmic', like the big bang . . . is there a difference?"

"No, there isn't a difference. Tell me why this word means something to you."

She answers, "Do you know, I once walked in on a friend. She was bent over a toilet bowl retching and I asked her if there was

73

anything that I might do to help. Which of us, myself or the vomit, was cataclysmic?"

"You were trying to be helpful."

"I was disruptive and tedious. She didn't need me. My sister told me that the only thing comparable to childbirth is retching; you know, when you can't stop and say, 'that's enough now,' and go home. All my life I've struggled to hold back a little, to pull back, to compose myself, but I'm not like that. I am cataclysmic. Like birth and retching."

In the afternoon, the children return. "Can I?" "Can I?" "Can I?" echo through the house and the expected "When you have finished your homework/lunch/cleaning your room . . ." follows suit. Would this be missed? Wasn't it what she wanted? Again she finds herself at the kitchen table – making time with the weekend paper. Why didn't she take this moment earlier? Now this casual retreat fills her with guilt.

When she announced Number One to her best friend, Kay, the question of "keeping it" was put forth.

"Yes," she'd replied, stunned by the query. The idea hadn't entered her mind to do otherwise.

Kay told her that she admired her strength of character – to take on such a commitment. "I couldn't do it . . . it is such a sacrifice and you are so young."

She wondered now if "it" had occurred to Nick.

Now the little "Can I's?" were her every moment – the "sacrifice" had multiplied.

Kay can't have babies and Iseult wonders how a woman must feel without the hysterical afters of a pregnancy . . . the brooding, selfless hormonal flux that encourages the body to instinctively want that feeling of fullness and rightness again. She can't quite remember wanting or willing any of the children. The waiting she does remember well. When the third baby arrived and it all became too exhausting, she remembered to turn her back to him at night.

Dermot McGarty

PLAYBACK

The street he commandeered,
With his solid walking cane,
An earthy face of a million passions,
Like prairie bison, hunted in vain.
Far away places were in his eyes,
Long dead lovers, lonely skies.
His tryst was wisdom,
His weapons were words,
From a wizened and toothless mouth
An exalted symphony surged.
Transmitted history with every touch,
Gifts of verbal snapshots,
Bellowed in a hush.
Of barefoot children in the summer rain,
Classroom brutality, I shared his pain.
Bare-knuckle street fighters armed to the teeth,
With honour and conviction, foreign to deceit.
Crossley tenders and dawn arrests,
Eucharistic congress, economic tests.
The hungry decades when thousands fled,
Death by consumption, hearts that bled.
A well-kept secret not revealed,
His very own golden rule.
Nine and a half decades of ordinary genius,
Draped across a frail, crumpled body,
Like some rare, sought after, sparkling jewel.

MELLIFONT |

Up a ladder, down a snake,
Better run for your life, jump in the lake,
When smart-assed meets sanguine,
In this game of give and take.
Reach for the stars, follow your own,
To history's final confluence,
Where your rebel heart still beats alone.

Your soul is most at rest, where ancient waters lap.
The spirits of the vanquished,
Gushing from the tap.
A promise of a second chance,
This yearning for a life re-born,
Where emptiness is everything.
An eternal longing, forever and forlorn.

Barbara Smith

DEATH OF THE INNOCENT

Their sun-strewn bedroom hazed
with the scent of out-haled alcohol,
tiny dust motes spiralled, caught
in the slanting draught of sunlight.

Grandma was gone to early mass.
I had gone into their room
in search of breakfast, a small child
lively and artless in large volume.

Granddad huddled in the many-layered
marital bed. Above the brown-barred
bedstead, a picture stood to.
Edwardian starch, patricians
ceding triumph to the future.

Grandma returned, suited and gloved.
I told her:
"Granddad won't wake up!"

Her eyes snapped shut like tomb slabs
her face curious in its closed-ness
"Here," she said,
"Have a bowl of Rice Krispies."

What sound remorse:
the heavy tock
of the mantel clock,
or the faint popping
of the rice in milk?

SHARP GROUND FROST |

The moon lies broken
as smatters of glass beside
the tin can hulk of a car.

It's cold, bone cold as I
scrunch across the courtyard
of memories, cauled

in a reflection pool.
Glass glints catch the eyes'
peripheries. This is no place

for a snail's trail, gone cold.
Safety has fled into the smear
of moonshadow. Blow cold,

East wind in the neap of spring;
tide to the imperfect puddle
of remembrance.

| SHOPPING TROLLEY

No frills shopping experience

The trolley that a man gave me
he had used to push around
his middle-aged contemplations
past the coffee and the tea
and toiletries.
He went for the TVs —
bargain of the week!

I used the trolley to push
my two and a half years
of fuddled frustration.
Concentrating on porridge
and packed lunches
with variety but no spice.

The trolley I gave in turn
to a tartan wheelie bag woman
She zoomed in on it;
her basics to buy
with her weekly pension.

That trolley saved us all
from fumbling with
our spare change.

Helen Curley

THE WHEELS ON THE BUS

Why do they always sit beside me? Every time I get on the bus it happens. You try to duck out of their gaze, you put your bag on the empty seat beside you, but up they march with the same stupid, bold stare – the one the rest of us know isn't on – and shout: "Anyone sitting here?"

But in they barge, sitting beside you . . . in your space.

They know you're too polite, too . . . well . . . normal – with your nice clothes, clean face – to risk raised voices. You won't put an argument when they start talking at you, you'll just try to get further into your nice winter coat, all the while praying that, at the next stop, they'll get the feck off.

And which, do you think, are worst? The drunks or the religious nuts? I'm hard pushed to find a choice between them – you just can't predict what they'll say or do next, can you?

I had a drunk religious nut sat beside me on the way to Dublin once who had the cheek to ask me:

"You wouldn't have change for a cup of tea?"

I gave him something for his troubles, to which he replied:

"God bless you, love."

And here's where I made my mistake. I said:

"He ain't blessing nobody."

And so I had to put up with a bus journey of a lecture that rambled into every corner of that misbegotten's mind and back again. I asked him to shut up and leave me alone but it just made him go on more.

But I don't understand why everyone was looking at *me* and why the bus driver put *me* off. Could they not see it was the fruitcake beside me?

It's not as if I can avoid these people. I have to travel on the bus. Besides, I have the free travel pass.

And then, there's psychiatrists. Always going on about the conversations you have on buses. Always putting labels on you. "Paranoid schizophrenic" indeed! I mean these people couldn't be a figment of a person's imagination, could they?

Roger Hudson

CAREER FOR SADISTS

It's a great game for sadists
This novel writing
He says
You just think up a load of characters
And put them through hell
No-one to stop you
No cops out gunning for you
No courts waiting to jail you
Got it made

Mr Nice Guy, family, home, cosy wife, kids
Humiliate the bugger
Boss, colleagues, neighbours
All got it in for him
Rows, arguments, crises of conscience, temptations to incest
You name it

He fights back
– Give the sod a chance –
So make them demote him, sack him,
Beat him up, rob his house, rape his wife

Wey hey!
Is this power or is this power?
God never had it so good.

Ah, he's an old softie, says the woman next
That's boring mental stuff
Writing scripts for slasher movies, that's the thing
No hard work making rounded complex characters
Just nice ordinary college grads
Scare the shit out of 'em
And let Mr Nasty cut 'em to bits
It wasn't me, Your Honour
He's just a character I invented

OK. You're only deskchair sadists
No-one really gets hurt
But doesn't it bother you?
All those proxy sadists
Or are they masochists identifying with the hero
Sitting out there reading those books
Viewing those films
Getting their kicks
From your sadistic subconscious creativity?

| THE NAMELESS ONES

On a crowded beach
a child's voice cries
in panic at some minor mishap

"Mammy!"

A hundred female heads turn

"Daddy!"

a hundred males
rise to their feet to look

"No, not mine", the thought

and settle back to relax
the child is someone else's worry
who emerges to fuss or slap or admonish guiltily

Who are these many-headed monsters
Mommy, mummy, mum, ma
Daddy, dada, dad, pop, da
this nameless horde
sacrificing individuality
to the anonymity
pseudonymity
of universal parenthood?

INFECTIOUS |

A happy smiling drunk
We don't know
Approaches our table
Smiles an infectious smile

Infected
We smile back

Extends a hand
We shake
An incoherent name
We give ours

An incoherent joke
He laughs
An infectious laugh

Infected
We laugh and go on laughing
Through all the incoherent drunken gibberish
So jolly and well-spirited

A total nothing conversation
That lifts our spirits with pure good humour

But we're pleased when he goes back to his friends
Not being drunk enough ourselves
To speak this language
With assurance
Not knowing when his mood may change
As happens sometimes
With drunks

Mary K Moore

BLACKBERRIES

The blackberries are out. In the hedgerows on the back road, branches are heavy with massy clusters of fruit, ripe for the picking. I pluck a handful and place them in my mouth. They burst on my tongue and in their sweetness I taste again the autumns of my childhood. Sunday drives with my father to his home place of Tenacre, County Wexford, to visit Uncle Shane and Aunt May.

Their yellow and red Shell garage sign hangs high over the road, visible for several hundred yards before the house. Uncle Shane is leaning against the petrol pump, and he waves at us as we drive up. Even on Sunday he's wearing his familiar brown garage overalls, oil-stained and baggy, the open flap of a squashed packet of Sweet Afton sticking out of his breast pocket.

He and my father share a passion for cars and motorbikes, anything to do with engines. Uncle Shane is rebuilding an old steam threshing engine in a shed behind the garage. The two brothers go off to inspect progress, while Aunt May shoos me into her warm kitchen, where she's baking apple tarts and preparing fruit for jam.

I ask her if I can go and pick blackberries in the field behind the house, bound as it was on three sides by ditches thick with blackberry, blackcurrant and gooseberry bushes. It seemed a vast adventure playground for a town-raised child like me.

So, armed with a milk can, and with strict instructions to fill it to the brim with fruit, my nine-year-old self sets off along the far ditch, plucking and eating, plucking and eating, until my mouth and hands are stained carmine red and my fingernails are black and pitted with seeds.

Back in the kitchen, Aunt May tut-tuts at the state of my hands and makes me wash them with red carbolic soap, and scrub my nails with a wire brush. "Can't send you home to your mother looking like that, can we?!"

Afterwards, she tips my can of blackberries, along with the rest, into a big old-fashioned skillet pot, on top of the range, and stirs in a measured quantity of sugar and water. Soon, the aroma of the simmering fruit fills the whole house, heady, pungent, like the port wine my father drank at Christmas.

Later, when the mixture cools and thickens, Aunt May ladles it out carefully into a sieve lined with a muslin cloth, and the jam, a glossy purple black, is then pressed through into an enamel mixing bowl beneath.

A gleaming row of newly washed jam jars sparkle in the sunlight on the windowsill, Aunt May having scrubbed and buffed each one as carefully as if they were her best crystal glasses.

As a special treat, she allows me to help her pour the jam into the jars, sealing each one with a disc of butter paper pressed down lightly on the top. "Careful now, Mary, there's a good girl," she says. "Let it sit gently. We want to seal it now, not drown it!" and we both laugh.

When the work is done, I'm allowed to sit in Uncle Shane's high-backed wing chair beside the range. It's deep and comforting and I tuck my legs right in under me and sink back into its sagging middle. Hiding behind the arm-rests, I pretend I can't be seen and imagine I'm Alice in Wonderland growing smaller and smaller as the furniture around me grows bigger.

When Uncle Shane comes in from the shed with my father, he claims his chair and I go and sit on a stool by the Aga. Aunt May hands each of us a plate of steaming hot apple tart, straight from the oven, juice bubbling up through the slits in the pastry, golden crust glistening with castor sugar. "Get that down ye!" Uncle Shane says. "That'll put hairs on your chest, girl!" But later at home when I look, I can't find any at all, and wonder why my parents laugh so much when I tell them.

A walk on the back road in autumn. Savouring a handful of blackberries plucked from a roadside ditch. Nature's bounty recalling a day in my childhood from more than four decades ago, a memory long stored and now revisited.

The blackberries are out . . .

Keith Roe

A SMILE THAT NEVER LEAVES

They pull up rrrrrr
It's about to begin and beep,
it's started and off they go.
110mph corners, 175mph straights
6, 9, 15 . . . But where is 45?

Then it happens. The Black Flag
and "Oh God, it's him."
Even though he raced for his life
he eventually flew to his death

A previous memory comes into mind.
A slight glance in his direction
to see his everlasting smile.
A dumb smile but still made sense.

The coffin closed, the cries opened
and into a building full of helpers.
Her speech began but was beaten by tears.

I remember sitting, wishing
it would end
so I could remember my lost friend.

FAINT BLACK BLOSSOMS |

Withered and torn
you stand in my garden
proud of your devilish black stare
cold and grim
naked and bare.
Your eyes and teeth
are gems to my eyes.
Wolf's eyes. Sharp and exact.

The gentle summer rain
holds no bearing on your position.
Still strong and bold
fighting the weight of this liquid salvation.
A thirst for the one thing that is a weight
on your dear petals.
So overpowering and creased.

Now the sun of autumn
strips you of your annual profit.
Will it break you?
You shiver and tremble but never give in.
The determination of a skunk.
Never let go.

Winter has killed your kin
and soaked your delicate skin.
But you still stand there
God to the ground.
Soon your end nears
I will not shed any tears
until another year.
My faint black blossom.

Kate Monaghan

LIVING ON THE STREETS

I stand here, people walk past me,
They see me but avoid my eyes,
Is there something wrong with me?
I don't belong to anyone,
Nothing seems real,
It feels like it's a dream but it's not,
I hear their feet stamp,
I will never be one of them.

I sit there trying to smile but I can't,
I lie here but people walk past my body,
They still think I should not be here,
I will be here until my body rots away,
Then for once I won't be judged
And I will be happy.

TOGETHER AND APART

I can't get away from you, you're everywhere,
when I'm awake I see you,
when I close my eyes I see you
Go Away!

I wish you would just go away,
Leave me alone scream in my dreams,
I wish night and day that you would leave me alone.

Then you are gone,
you disappeared
I didn't know what to do,
you were not in my dreams, you were not in my head,
Then I realised I loved you.

Betty Glennon

DARREN'S JOURNEY

Driving along smartly, Darren was quite relaxed as he hummed along to the radio.

Motorway traffic isn't too bad this evening, he thought, tapping his fingers on the steering wheel in time to the music. Then he noticed red brake lights coming on in the distance. The traffic began slowing, slowing more, then it stopped, moved again and stopped again. One lane moved a little, then the other lane moved a little. Then that familiar feeling, part dread, part excitement, in his stomach as he started to realise that there might have been an accident.

Not that he wanted anybody to get hurt, but, oh yes, the buzz he got when he saw the wrecked cars, the Garda car, the ambulance or the fire brigade was better than the best night out. His excitement grew as the cars inched along. He could feel his tongue stick to the roof of his mouth as the adrenaline surged through his veins. His hands clenched tightly on the steering wheel as the traffic moved a little faster.

Then, on his left-hand side, he noticed some debris but, alas, no cars, no ambulance, no Garda car and no fire brigade. It had all just been cleared away. Disappointed and annoyed, he jerked the steering wheel to pull into the fast lane. But, unnoticed by him, the traffic in the outside lane had already increased speed.

As he glanced too late into the rearview mirror, a truck loomed and that familiar feeling, dread, excitement. There was going to be an accident. The traffic ground to a halt again. A smashed car was there, his, the Garda car was back too, the ambulance had been called, even the fire brigade was coming with the cutting equipment but, unfortunately, Darren had already involuntarily left the scene.

Or was his spirit still hovering, watching one last time – an accident?

| LOST AT SEA

Again they stand
Again they stare
Looking to sea for the missing one
Dark approaches, the boats return
At first light the search resumes

Dawn Staudt

ICE SKATER

Long ago
   Winter's glow
Little girl
   Took a whirl
On the ice
   It was nice . . .
Ice Skater
   God made her!

       Slow at first
          That was worst
       With the years
          She lost fears
       Moving fast
          Never last
       Ice and snow
          Face aglow
       Heat and sweat
          Body wet
       Heart racing
          No pacing

Moving on
   Winter pond
Skate along
   River long
Snow and weeds
   Skater speeds
Go, go, go
   Never slow
Speed skater
   God made her!

Freedom now
　　This is how
Wind in ear
　　Feel God near
Feel the thrill
　　Don't mind chill
Sometimes fall
　　Like them all
Up she'd get
　　Clothes all wet
Not hurt long
　　Skating on
Best outside
　　Wind, snow, glide!

Years pass by . . .
　　How they fly
Mother now
　　Show kids how
After all
　　She recalls . . .
Ice Skater
　　God made her!

Inside rinks
　　Fun she thinks
Round and round
　　With the sound
Music blasts
　　Skating fast
Beat for beat
　　Move her feet
Moving fast
　　Like the past
Days of old
　　Skating bold

Show them how
    "Watch me now!"
Heat and sweat
    Body wet
Heart racing
    No pacing
Feel the thrill
    Don't mind chill
Sometimes fall
    Like them all…

Now it's worse . . .
    Age the curse!
Hit the ice . . .
    Not so nice . . .
Black and blue . . .
    Ouch, boo hoo . . .
Pain for weeks . . .
    Move with squeaks . . .
Fall apart . . .
    Not too smart . . .
Body slows . . .
    Now she knows:

Forty-four
    Skate no more!

A SOUL NOBLE –
THE CRIME GLOBAL

The homeless young man in Drogheda

I didn't ever really know him,
Though often I saw him in the town.
There was a radiance about him,
Though it seemed life had taken him down.

One would see him sitting on the ground,
Most often dishevelled and unclean.
Through these ragged conditions of life,
He greeted you with a smile that gleamed.

Sometimes I would give him things to eat,
Though I know I could have done much more.
What holds back all the good intentions?
Why is it that we can't help the poor?

Sometimes his face had cuts or bruises.
Sometimes he laid on the street "out cold".
My heart broke and I felt so helpless.
"A loss" for all who passed to behold.

Such a loss of human dignity –
The spirit created so noble.
Who's to blame for the loss of this soul?
We all are – and the crime is global.

Then the news came that he had passed on.
Though now set free, I was sad he'd died.
Days later on the ground by the bank
I saw flowers for him and I cried.

I'll go now to his memorial.
Prayers for his blessed young soul I'll say.
In the next life his soul is with God.
With Him his radiant smile will stay.

But let us here remember his smile
And try better to do what we can
For those whose life is different than ours –
Do it in memory of this young man.

Damien Somerville

MALFUNCTION

What's the matter with me?
Another day spreads isolation
Into an intellect that malfunctions.
Thoughts, words and expressions
Entangled like prey in a spider's web.
Powerless to unravel its yarn of despair.

What day is it?
Futile questions measured with hollow responses.
Precise explanations
Acknowledged with vacant glances.
A willing decaying faculty
Unable to conceive past, present or future.

What time is it?
Twilight extinguished by darkness
Invites only a restless sleep.
Warm softness of the down
Allures the faint gentle voice
Whispering words of humble gratitude.

When are they coming over?
Pondering what lies ahead
As the sunlight searches a shaded room
For the repetitions of yesterday.
As today's fading memories
Will have dissolved by tomorrow.

Please take me home.
Drapes partially drawn, window ajar.
Sweet tranquil chant of bird song
Descends from stems of wild lilac
Penetrating a laconic breathless sigh
Entwined with the ultimate refrain.

A RACEHORSE NAMED DROGHEDA

An equine star with Drogheda's name
Achieved the ultimate in Grand National fame.
Birch and bramble were left in a state
On a March day in eighteen ninety-eight.

During a snowstorm came into his own
Became a steeplechaser of great renown.
Prodigy carrying the silk of amber and black
When galloping around Aintree race track.

First past the post and cheers of joy
Affectionately greeted by his loyal stable boy.
Owners, trainers, punters alike
All sang his praises in cheerful voice.

Always graceful on the hoof
On turf lush and green,
The gallant hero rose to the test
At the age of seven gave his best.

Grazed and matured on pastures fine
Bordering near the banks of the Boyne,
If ever you tread on Dowth's wild gorse
Remember *Drogheda*, our famous race horse.

Nellie Brennan

CHILDHOOD MEMORIES

School holidays started the first week in July. It was a great thrill to wake up on a lovely sunny summer morning and not have to go to school. Holiday time was Babby house time.

My sister Isobelle, our friend Eliza and I always played together. We agreed that the first thing to do was to take a walk up the lane and pick out a nice site for our houses. Whoever was there first always got the best site. The one on the highest part of the bank, where all your treasures could be displayed without fear of the farmer's cows trampling on them, was the best place. Isobelle and I thought we'd be the first to mark out our sites, so we went up the lane early only to find that, as usual, Eliza was there before us and had got the best place.

We started to work, clearing the weeds and briars from the bank. The highest part was cleared by scraping the clay away to form a shelf. This spot was to be the dresser and the whole Babby house revolved around this space. Next started the cleaning and building of walls. The house consisted of two rooms, a kitchen and a sitting room. The walls were made by sweeping the dust of the lane into lines with handfuls of leaves pulled off the ash tree which grew on the opposite side of the lane and which gave us shelter in the event of a shower of rain.

Once the walls were in place, the furniture was installed. Four stones in the centre of the room supported a piece of wood, usually the top of a tea chest, to make a table. Around this structure were placed four flat stones which were used for seats. Then the kitchen was fitted out. A ring of stones and a handful of sprigs made an ideal fire. The ditches were scoured to find the remains of an old saucepan or kettle to place on the fire. The delph used in the kitchen consisted of broken cups, plates and saucers. The more decorative they were the more valuable were these "cheneys".

The larder was also stocked up. The seeds of docks made pretend dry tea. The main foods were sorrel, haws, sloes, dandelions and wild garlic. All these foods were edible but, looking back now, it's no wonder we never needed laxatives or had worms. Fresh supplies were gathered every morning. Dandelions and dog roses were the favourite flowers for the vases. Ferns tied to a long piece of stick made a bisom for everyday cleaning.

There were no bedrooms in the Babby house. Now that our rooms were furnished and we were all as dusty as engine drivers, we were all set to begin visiting and partying. We took turns at visiting each others' houses and having tea. This took us up to lunchtime, when we all traipsed home to be fed. Having had our hands and faces washed at lunchtime, we each looked a bit more respectable in the afternoon. A Marietta biscuit or a piece of bread and jam saved from lunch made a tasty snack for afternoon tea.

We hated the days when the farmer was grazing his cows in the field farther down the lane because the cows were always taken home to the farmyard to be milked and, cows being cows, would drop their pats right in the middle of the sitting room. Having been grazing on fresh grass, they could leave a deposit in all three houses. This was overcome by sprinkling loads of dust over the mess and sweeping it onto a rusty piece of tin battered with a stone into the shape of a shovel. Dirty little devils, you might say, but we were as healthy as wild ducks and happy into the bargain. We were never bored. We hadn't even heard of the word.

The best feast in the Babby house was a young turnip, snigged on the bars of the field gate and then scraped with a piece of broken delph and wiped on the bottom of your dress, which could very often be used to wipe your nose as well. There were no tissues, kitchen rolls or anti-bacterial wipes in the 1940s.

We also went for walks along the lane. We learned where all the birds nested, what colour their eggs were and how many each bird laid. We watched every day for the scaldies to emerge from the shells and kept an eye on them as they learned to fly. The little birds fought with each other in the nests and there was sometimes unrest in the three houses on the lane as well. Coming towards evening as tiredness set in, sometimes tempers became short. It would take very little provocation to start a full-scale row. When this happened, we'd pull each other's hair and roll about on the dusty lane. Then everyone went home, each one shouting, "I'm going to tell my mammy on you". It's a good job our mothers never got involved in our squabbles because the next day we would be as thick as thieves again.

We were never allowed to play up the lane after six o'clock. Each one played in their own backyard. Next morning about ten o'clock, Eliza would be outside our gate shouting, "Are you coming up the lane to play Babby house?"

She would have her doll with her, so Isobelle and I would grab our Raggy Maggies, and head for the lane after saying goodbye to our mother and telling her where we were going and promising not to fight. Since the territorial rights had been settled the day before, each one headed for their own house. There would be a busy morning ahead of us, repairing the damage done by the cows as they were put out to graze for the day.

The Babby house lasted all summer, although we did not spend all our time playing there. Sometimes we caught bees in jam jars and some days we went to the sea and had picnics and caught pinkeens, but that's a chat for another day.

Dermot Fairclough
(The Country Fella)

I AM PROUD OF
OUR TOWN

Our town, I own, is not a common place;
Here people's tongues accenting words the same
Speak good or evil, curse or pray, and yet
It's not common, when I hear its name.

But when its houses gave me first a home
To start a voice in, or to touch a face,
Naming me names, now beauty's alphabet,
I name that town before another place.

It was old before some cities were born.
A medieval and monastic town it stands
Divided by the Boyne, united by Saint Oliver
This old town where I was born.

ABIDE IN PEACE |

Where trickling beads of water fall
From cliffs o'er hung with pale green moss,
Where cheery cuckoo pipes her call,
There calm is found from cankering cross.

On Ireland's shores where rugged rocks
Are buffeted and drenched with spray,
Where caverns echo forth sea shocks,
Where the thrushes trill goodbye to day,

Where breezes blow in valleys deep,
The sun sinks down the mountain steep.
In arms where baby loves to creep,
In all these ways, sweet peace, sweet peace.

Joan Moran

JULIA

Liz climbed the stairs, her heavy body panting with breathlessness. In her left hand was a dishcloth which itself was performing feats of an athletic nature as Liz swung her arms to and fro with the process of steering her body upwards at a speed over and beyond the limits of her own endurance.

"Holy Mother of God!" she shouted. "Will there never be an end to it all? It would take a bomb the size of the one that fell on Hiroshima to get that daughter of mine out of her bed each day."

Liz entered the bedroom. "Jesus Christ!" she swore (in a broad Dublin accent), "the bloody bomb has already hit the place."

She looked around; things were getting worse not better. She sighed deeply, giving in to despair. Next, her eyes fell upon the object of her upstairs flight: the bed and its occupant.

Liz raised one hand to her brow to steady herself as she studied the disarray before her eyes. She examined the unruly bed linen, prodding the clothes here and there as she tried to locate the body position of her daughter. Try as she would, she could not make out the head from the feet, and this prevented her giving a good puck to alert the sleeper.

"Julia! Julia! Julia!" she shouted at the top of her voice.

At last the blankets showed signs of movement. Very, very slowly a long drawn-out low complaining moan echoed ever so slightly. Liz, still grasping the dishcloth, was seething with exasperation. Placing her hands upon her hips, biding her time for the moment her daughter's head would emerge, so that she could start an emotional onslaught. The awaited moment never arrived; instead the motion of the bedclothes settled down once again.

There was a pregnant pause as silence filled the air.

Akin to the frightening roar of a lion, Liz raged, "Get your lazy carcass out of that bed, NOW!"

This time, a mop of hair, attached to a head of course, made its appearance.

Blinking fiercely at the glare from the sunlight entering the window, Julia tried to focus and gather her senses. Through bleary eyes, she looked upon her mother's angry features.

"Ah, Ma," she said bleatingly, the agony of the world's problems lying upon her eighteen-year-old shoulders, "It's a Bank Holiday. I don't have to go to work today!"

Marie McSweeney

PATHWAYS

As if we were reluctant travellers loitering here
we chose to move along a path
that has no clear aim,
but only earth ahead, coiling into a tangled undergrowth.

Purpose is a fickle place that slips away
when we search it out, and we lose direction,
shuffle madly as we stray around a maze
of wet days, and nights without the solace of moon or stars.

Our boots and clothes are tattered now,
fatally frayed about the edges, and we cannot see
how sky and sea become snarled, and trees retrench
while we venture forward in this stubborn spinney.

But oh, the grace of it, to stumble upon sinewy headlands
and scorched hills, to embrace this sparse landscape
as it fans out before us, with no swank to it,
but only heat swelter and haze and struggling whin,

barbs ready to breathe discreet designs along our skin.

HUBBLE |

I am Hubble's troubled eye
which charts a wayward track through space,
strays into the outer wilderness
with almost no way home.

I am Hubble's ear, bent to the faint
strains of covert, cosmic symphonies,
longing to hear soft, sibilant
voices whisper in my wake.

I am Hubble's right arm,
wrapped around the universe,
while the other rigid, long-fingered
probes the darkness beyond for hidden worlds.

I am the lonely heart of Hubble.
I bleed in the bleakness around me.

I am the joker from Eden.
I am the weeping clown.

PHOTOGRAPHING A SUPERNOVA

Dodging the draw and drag
of a black hole

my lens telescopes
through space

to fix the final,
balletic dance

of a dying star,
two faltering clusters

searing the darkness,
like an embryonic

cell dividing,
but with the future reversed,

white heart shivering
in the cold of it,

needing our eyes only to verify
its dark energy,

we are star stuff
contemplating the stars.

Shane Fagan

A HOME FOR BISTO

When Max, our beloved old border collie, finally passed away, a dark cloud of gloom seemed to hang over our household for ages. I'd never known a time without Max. For all of my ten years, he'd been my playmate, my protector, and my loyal and constant companion. It was on a bright windswept afternoon in late November when this enduring relationship came to a sudden and traumatic end.

The Da and I had been raking up leaves in the orchard at the back of our house while Max bounded about with his usual enthusiasm. Suddenly, old Max seemed to stagger. Seconds later, he was lying prone beneath the spreading canopy of the big chestnut tree while a robin watched in silent empathy at the spot. For an instant, the two of us stood transfixed, but as the jaded brown and gold leaves fluttered downward and came to rest upon his lifeless body, the tragic reality struck home: my best friend had gone – gone for ever!

Later that afternoon, close to where he had fallen, my tearful Mother watched silently as the Da and I laid old Max to rest. When we'd finished, the Da placed a large flat stone to mark the spot.

As we made our way back to the house, there was an unfamiliar tremor in the Da's voice as he murmured, "Timmy me lad, that's the last dog we'll ever have!" I didn't answer, but he'd that look in his eye – the look that told me that he meant every word. Up until now, being an only child had had many advantages, but, in the months that followed, the opposite seemed to be the case and my days were filled with episodes of painful loneliness.

During those times, my mind would play cruel little tricks on me. Sometimes, I imagined I could see Max bounding up and down the long winding avenue that led to our old house. Other times, he would be dozing contentedly in his favourite sunny spot right behind the hen house.

One rainy May afternoon the following year, I was aimlessly kicking a tin can in front of me as I dawdled home from school. By this time, my feelings for old Max had receded to a hallowed place somewhere deep in my memory, and life was good again. It was then that fate decided to take a hand.

Cowering at the side of the deserted country road, looking drenched and forlorn, was a little brown dog of the mongrel variety. When I stooped down to pet him, he rolled his big dewy eyes beguilingly and offered a bony rain-sodden paw. From that moment, all thoughts of what the Da had said about never having another dog evaporated completely from my head, and scooping up the shivering little body in my arms, I ran the rest of the way home. As I did so, inspired by his colour, I decided to "christen" the trembling little waif – from now on, he would be known as "Bisto".

When I lifted the latch on the back door and entered the kitchen, a stunned silence greeted my arrival. The Da was halfway through his afternoon mug of tea and nearly scalded himself with the shock. Mother was standing at the kitchen table, rolling out pastry. Then the Da started, "Didn't I tell you, Timmy, that there would be no more dogs after Max?"

He then pointed to the door and was about to order me to take Bisto right back to where I found him, when a discreetly raised eyebrow from Mother seemed to mollify his anger.

"Just keep him out of my way," the Da muttered, as he brushed past me on his way back to the cowshed.

Now, I had to admit, things were beginning to look a little unpromising but at least Mother seemed to be on my side. I figured that, by helping Bisto keep a low profile, the Da would eventually come around and accept the paw of friendship from our little canine lodger.

In the days that followed, a warm camaraderie quickly blossomed between Bisto and me, and it was plain to see that the little stray had an abundance of very endearing qualities. These very qualities, I had no doubt, would have Bisto in the Da's good books in no time at all. Just the same, as a precautionary measure, I continued to keep a watchful eye on Bisto's low profile.

As our relationship grew ever closer, it transpired that a new and worrying element was beginning to become apparent; Bisto, I was slowly discovering, had a character trait of a less endearing nature – a recurring tendency to break wind! At first, I looked upon this as nothing more than a passing malady, something that in time would disappear.

Nothing could have been further from the truth. Several weeks later, and with still no let up in this anti-social behaviour, I was forced to the inevitable conclusion – Bisto was, in fact, a full-time windbreaker!

Could this, I wondered, have been the reason why Bisto had come to be a vagrant in the first place? Whether it was or not, I sensed that tricky times lay ahead; now, more than ever, Bisto needed to be kept well out of the Da's way.

It was on the following Sunday, as the three of us sat down to dinner, that Bisto really put his paw in it! Somehow, unknown even to me, he'd managed to sneak in to the kitchen and had secreted himself under the table. Not only that, but he was giving a virtuoso performance right under the Da's nose!

When the Da yanked up the tablecloth and discovered the source of the unpleasant updraught, well, I just knew the game was up and that the unfortunate Bisto's eviction was at hand.

"Get that Bisto fella outa here," the Da demanded, "I never want to see his rear end in this house again!"

The Da had that same look in his eyes, and I knew that any further petitions on behalf of my four-legged friend would prove to be futile. Scooping up the startled Bisto lest something even more drastic befall him, I scampered down the avenue toward the road. Instinctively, I started to run in the direction of old Jem Rooney's cottage.

Old Jem had worked as ploughman for more than forty years and now, in his retirement, he devoted all of his time to his beloved rose garden. He was also a good friend – someone to whom I could turn in times of crisis.

I knew that Jem had been feeling very lonesome since his wife, Rosie, had passed away some twelve months earlier. I hoped that maybe, just maybe, he would accept into his home the trembling little stray that I was clutching to my chest.

When Jem opened his door to my knock, he grasped the situation immediately, and his reply to my tremulous request made my heart leap with delight.

"Of course I'll give the little fellow a home, Timmy," he beamed, "sure he'll be great company for me."

Deep down, I knew that this was the proper time to alert Jem about Bisto's little "weakness" but, try as I might, the words just wouldn't come.

For the next day or two, I was elated about my successful visit to Jem, but as the week wore on, worrying new clouds began to appear on the horizon. What if Bisto's little problem was putting a bit of a strain on Jem's hospitality? I tried to banish the thought. After all, old Jem had spent nearly half a century walking behind a pair of hard-pulling Clydesdale plough horses; compared to the velocity of their wind breaking, anything little Bisto might emit would probably go unnoticed by old Jem. I simply couldn't convince myself, however, no matter how hard I tried, and the spectre of yet another sorry eviction loomed ever larger in my head. Every day, I expected a rather vexed Jem to appear at our door dangling a distraught Bisto by the scruff of the neck.

By the time Saturday had arrived and there were still no developments, I could endure the tension no longer. That very afternoon found me, once again, lifting the latch of Jem's front gate.

Racing up the winding, herbaceous-bordered path that led to the cottage, I suddenly skidded to a halt. Unfolding before my eyes was a reassuring vista the likes of which I could never have anticipated.

Jem was reclining in his favourite rickety old garden chair, and, more importantly, nestling contentedly between his well-polished brown boots, was the dozing Bisto. Framed by a profusion of rose blossoms, they were in blissful togetherness, as they relaxed peacefully in the hot afternoon sun.

A new confidence had added a lilt to my voice when I jolted Jem from his serene summer slumber, "How are you two getting along?" I enquired brightly. Jem's face lit up, and reaching down a toil-worn leathery hand, he gently stroked Bisto's ear. "We're getting along famously," he chuckled, "sure wouldn't I be lost without him."

For over an hour, we chatted and laughed while Bisto, still luxuriating in the shade of Jem's ample trouser bottoms, looked from one to the other. As we talked in the deliciously warm sunshine, an inexpressible relief was permeating my very being. All those nagging fears, which had tormented me so relentlessly, were now melting away – like summer vapours toward an unblemished sky.

When at last I prepared to take my leave, I stooped to inhale the scent of an exquisite old yellow tea rose.

"What's this one called, Jem?" I enquired brightly. "It has a beautiful fragrance." Strangely, the beaming smile on the old ploughman's weather-beaten face seemed to falter and, when he answered, I would almost swear that I spotted Bisto wink!

"That one's called Peace, Timmy," Jem disclosed ruefully, "but to my life-long regret, I know little of its fragrance; you see, the good Lord never blessed me with a sense of smell . . ."

Steve Downes

HAPPY VALENTINE

I never believed in love
a fictitious state invented by Disney
Hallmark
and *Cosmopolitan*

As a divine gift from above
it would be bestowed on all
handsome men
thin girls
and non-threatening gays

But now with the sniper
hindsight of age I can count
the ways in which these
pearls of delusion have proved unwise
rotten to their silvery core

For each Adam there
is not an Eve
no rib is given to all
some get an elbow
most have to settle

Biological clocks edging
them to call time on sexual exuberance
and name any Adam or Eve
a life lover

If I believed in love
I wouldn't find much solace
in the words of poets
they tend to lie

THROW IT OUT |

At what point do you
call for help?
When is it too late?

Who do you ask?

What if they refuse?

Where is the bottom of the barrel
double barrel to the mouth
                        surely too far
Razor blade to a vein
a wrist risk in vanity
Who would care
if the fallen falls a little further
How deep into twilight
before darkness consumes
How much wreckage must there be
before all in here becomes rubbish

Throw it out
when in doubt
throw it all out

MORTGAGE MORALISE |

Get on
get on
get on the ladder
shaky ladder
it's got two bathrooms
one sweet
if you have to relieve your bladder
no surprise

when you see the price
half a million a concrete box
"oh that'll be nice!"
Beg your bank to take
you in debt
we own your life until your death
have some kids
we want theirs too
and 150% more than we're due
Don't complain
you're on the first rung
not high enough yet
to get yourself hung

| COMMUTER WIDOW

Trainspotting
isn't fun
not when she's dead tired
arms of jelly
ears full of tears
      baby wants
      baby wants
pick the kids up
from school
strawberry jam
sandwiches uneaten
traffic jam
      ma I'm hungry
      baby wants
      baby wants
make the dinner
bake the cake
bun in the oven
bending over
nightly shapes

the body pays the price
of newborn joy
      headache
joyless
thankless
throb
9 to 5
paced out
on the kitchen floor
supermarket
      chicken would be good
      baby wants sweets
5 o'clock
tick tock
train halfway
baby straps
double check
      throb
In at seven
should be six-thirty
commuter widow waits
for the daily rebirth of
a partnership
      what a day I've had luv
he shallowly sits
TV
dinner
bed
make the shapes
if both are able
      How did it come
      to this
nearly dawn
where's his tie
      I used to be a woman
intelligent
bright
outgoing

       he used to be a man
wide-eyed
unpredictable
caring
       no time to care now
we used to be together
in this
       this mess
baby just wants a hug

the question you didn't answer
what's left
?
When reality robs us of dreams
what do you see in me
lined
fatter
turning sour
at being cheated
and then depressed when
I realise I cheated myself
out of a better life
what's left
?
What do you see
when you look at me
settlement
or
excitement
is it still there
is it still detectable
after all that has passed
?

|

118

About the Contributors

Who are the 38 local contributors to this anthology? Seven are here by invitation – Drogheda's most nationally established poet Susan Connolly, who has seven published collections and won the Patrick and Katherine Kavanagh Fellowship in 2001, and well-known local poets John "Dixie" Nugent (two collections), Barbara Smith (work published in many poetry magazines and a collection on the way) and Marie McSweeney, a winner of the Francis McManus Short Story Award, whose stories, poems, essays and plays have been published in many periodicals, two books and performed on radio. Add to these Shane Fagan, whose stories have appeared on *Sunday Miscellany* and in *Ireland's Own* and other periodicals, and Oisin McGann, who is rapidly building a reputation as a prolific children's author with his growing list of published books, including the *Mad Grandad* series. Brian Quinn, best known locally as director of the Kayther Theatre Group, reveals another aspect to his creativity.

Another six have only recent connections with the group, appearing at our open sessions. All are still at school, representatives of a larger group of budding writers which meets lunchtimes at the Sacred Heart School. These are Kate Monaghan (first year), Shannon Walsh (third year), Ria Duff (sixth year), Keith Roe (sixth year, Gormanston College), Ciaran Hodgers (fifth year, St Joseph's) and Amy Hibbits (second year). The girls are all at Sacred Heart School. Ria recently completed the first novel in her *Knightly Chaos* Trilogy.

Everyone else is a past or present member of Drogheda Creative Writers. They range from Nuala Early, a regular contributor to the *Drogheda Independent*, who was a founding member of the writers' group 19 years ago, and Tom Winters, another long-serving and active member, editor of the *Old Drogheda Society Journal*, whose work also appears in the *Drogheda Independent* and other local and national periodicals, to those who have been with us for a year or less. These include Brian Langan, who works in publishing and has a published novel behind him, Helen Curley, who is working on a chick-lit novel, and Helen Cooney, a lecturer in literature at Trinity College, who has been delighted to discover that she too can write the complex poetry of her modernist idols.

Some, like Dermot McGarty, Betty Glennon, Joan Moran and Roger Hudson arrived here in recent years from Dublin and other parts of Ireland; some from other lands such as Dawn Staudt from America, Claudia Terry from Canada and Maggie Pinder from Australia. The majority, including Lillie Callan, Bridie Clarke, Damien Somerville, Maura McDonnell are born and bred in the Drogheda area, even if some have travelled away and returned.

In style, contributions range from the highly literary to community writing whose aim is to communicate memoirs as straightforwardly as possible. In subject, the writing varies from the humour of Jim Brady, John Doherty and Joan Moran to the piercing social analysis and cunning wordplay of Steve Downes's poems, from the deep-digging and skilful personality studies of prose writers Claudia Terry and award-winning Bernadette Smyth to the emotive and unpretentious prose poems of Paul Murray and beyond to the captivating childhood memories of Nellie Brennan and Mary Moore and the wry reflections of Teddy Doyle, Bridie Clarke and Lillie Callan.

There's a strong sense of place in much of the work, such as that by Damien Somerville, Dawn Staudt and Dermot McGarty, who use their outward surroundings as inspiration. Others turn inward for their subjects, as in the poems of Maura McDonnell. But, then, many of the writers here are delving into and drawing on their personal experience to bring us their own individual flashes of insight and observation in ways that illuminate and entertain, though Marie McSweeney alone has the courage to venture into the distant reaches of outer space. Only Dermot Fairclough is no longer with us, but we are pleased to include examples of his work.

This brief summary and this collection cannot do full justice to the creativity of the contributors. Many more of the contributors than indicated have had works published, broadcast or performed on stage, many have completed but so far unpublished poems, novels and plays. Steve Downes, for instance, has three poetry collections published and award-winning plays performed. Some have other creative achievements such as Paul Murray's photography and Teddy Doyle's painting. However, we hope this very readable collection gives some idea of the creativity of this highly creative town.

| About the Editors

Roger Hudson has worked in many areas of writing and editing – publicity, technical editing, careers literature, journalism, magazine editing and corporate video scripting. Since moving to Dublin from London 14 years ago and four years ago to Drogheda, his more creative work includes completion of a novel and filmscripts, writing and directing *Wordweaver,* a TV documentary about Benedict Kiely, and publishing a book of poetry, *Side-Angles,* with Steve Downes.

Maggie Pinder is an award-winning writer of literary erotica, and has over three dozen stories published in US and UK anthologies. As partner of Bushducks Global Adventures, she is the co-author of several backcountry travel books for the USA. Her photography appears in the award-winning documentary *Time After Time.* Maggie and her Irish partner spend half the year researching, writing and photographing around the world, and the other six months in Drogheda where she is an active member of DCW.

| Credits

Bernadette Smyth's *Kissing* won the Tobias Wolff Award for Fiction, 2004. It first appeared in the *Bellingham Review* (Washington, USA) in the spring of 2005.

Dixie Nugent's *The Balkans, The Tiger, Sadie,* and *Disco Flu* all first published in his collection *Miscellaneous Collectables.*

Arthur Sheridan's *Spider* previously published in *Dublin Stories* from Inkwell Writers Group, 2006

Barbara Smith's *Death of the Innocent* first published in *Agenda,* (UK), 2005.

Acknowledgements |

Drogheda Creative Writers would like to acknowledge the financial assistance of the Arts Office of Drogheda Borough Council, of Drogheda Concentrates, of Drogheda Credit Union and of the recently opened branch of Marks & Spencer in the Laurence Centre. Also Droichead Arts Centre for their ongoing support. Thanks must also go to our treasurer Tommy Winters for handling the finances and raising sponsorship and to Nuala Early for her efforts in publicising our activities, and Donald Mc Gann for layout and formatting assistance. The editors would also like to thank John Moloney for his cover design, Richard Moore for allowing us to use his painting of Peter Street in Drogheda for the cover, and Brian Langan for proof-reading the text so meticulously. Our gratitude especially to best-selling novelist Deirdre Purcell, the area's most well-known author, for providing the Introduction.

With grateful thanks to our sponsors:

Drogheda Borough Council   **Drogheda Concentrates**

Marks and Spencer

Drogheda Credit Union